STRUTS & FRETS

STRUTS & FRETS

& FRETS

JON SKOVRON

Amulet Books
New York

Library of Congress Cataloging-in-Publication Data

Skovron, Jon.
Struts and frets / by Jon Skovron.
p. cm.
Summary: Sammy wants to be a musician, as was his grandfather, but while the band he is in is self-destructing, Sammy is too distracted by his grandfather's decline and his confused feelings about his best friend to fix it—and his mother stays too busy to help.
ISBN 978-0-8109-4174-8
[1. Bands (Music)—Fiction. 2. Self-confidence—Fiction. 3. Interpersonal relations—Fiction. 4. Grandfathers—Fiction. 5. Single-parent families—Fiction. 6. Columbus (Ohio)—Fiction.] I. Title.

PZ7.S628393Str 2009
[Fic]—dc22
2008045925

Book design by Chad W. Beckerman

Printed and bound in U.S.A.
10 9 8 7 6 5 4 3 2 1

ABRAMS
THE ART OF BOOKS SINCE 1949

115 West 18th Street
New York, NY 10011
www.abramsbooks.com

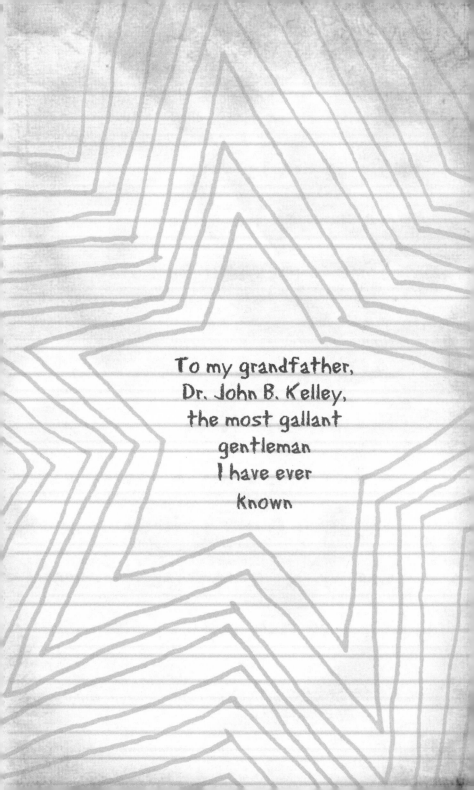

To my grandfather,
Dr. John B. Kelley,
the most gallant
gentleman
I have ever
known

Contents ⚡

Idiots Rule

1

Our band was called Tragedy of Reason. Or Tragedy of Wisdom. We hadn't decided yet. I liked "Reason" because it said how much it sucked to be the only thoughtful person in a crazy world. But our frontman, Joe, liked "Wisdom" because, he said:

"It just sounds cooler!"

We rehearsed at the Parks and Rec building downtown. It was an old dance studio, with slick wooden floors and tall mirrors on every wall, but I was pretty sure that no one had danced there for a long time. The mirrors were all smudged and cracked. The balance barre screwed into one wall was barely holding on, and only one flickering fluorescent light worked. The whole place felt like an abandoned set from one of those old '80s dance movies my mom liked to watch.

I had talked about the band name before rehearsal with Rick the bassist and TJ the drummer, and we had all agreed that "Reason" made more sense. But they didn't say anything now because they were afraid to piss off Joe.

Okay, okay. I was afraid to piss off Joe too. He was one of those guys who started shaving in junior high. He was almost two feet taller than Rick and me. He was about the same height as TJ, but TJ was a lanky, stooped hipster boy and Joe was a massive, pierced, steel-toe-boot-wearing, leather-and-all-the-crazy-spikes metal dude. And he wasn't one of those "Oh, once you get to know him, he's such a softie" kind of guys. No, once you got to know him, you realized that deep down, he was even scarier.

The problem was that even though I was scared of Joe, I had a hard time keeping my mouth shut. So I said, "But what does that even mean? Tragedy of *Wisdom*? It's like, doesn't it suck to understand things? Who thinks that? And we may be a lot of things, but we're definitely not wise."

"Hey, speak for yourself," said Rick, joking to lighten the mood. Nobody would mistake Rick for being wise. He was such a *dude*. People who weren't his friend might have called him a burnout. The kind of guy who had a permanent dazed expression and bed head.

"Right," I said, "like huffing Dust-Off is really wise."

"Ouch," mumbled TJ.

"Only that one time," said Rick. "Just to see if it worked."

"You really did that?" asked TJ as he brushed aside his mop of brown hair. He was always doing that. Pretty much anytime I talk about him, imagine him doing that. "Didn't you know that it can freeze your brain?"

"Not at the time, of course," said Rick.

"You *totally* knew," I said. "Because I told you right before you did it."

"Oh." Rick shrugged. "Well, you know I kinda tune you out a lot, Sammy, so I probably just missed it."

"You tune him out too?" said TJ. "Oh, good. I was worried that I was the only one."

"Ha-ha," I said. "Just wait until you're about to step off a cliff or something and I'm trying to warn you but—"

"SHUT UP, YOU IDIOTS!"

Joe.

"Listen, this isn't some kind of pukey, whiny, emo band!" he said. "This is hardcore!" He illustrated his point by kicking the metal trash can across the room. It hit the far wall with a sharp clang, and fast-food wrappers and a half-full drink cup spilled out onto the floor. He waited for a minute in silence, looming over us, with his big, meaty fists clenched and ready.

"It can't sound like some faggot-ass wannabe shit," he said.

"It has to sound cool! We have to be cool! And until I can get a *real* band who actually *are* cool, the three of you are just going to have to try really hard to *seem* cool." He paced back and forth in front of us like a rhino looking for a reason to charge. "Any problems with that?"

No one said anything.

"Well?" he said. Then he stopped directly in front of me and glared.

"No, Joe," I said, feeling like the punk bitch he thought I was. "No problems."

"Don't forget," said Joe, starting to pace again. "I'm the one who started this band. I'm the one who knows the guy who runs this Parks and Rec building and gets us this killer rehearsal space. I'm the one who scored the practice drum kit so TJ doesn't have to lug his own kit down here all the time." He stopped pacing directly in front of me again, but right up close this time. His breath smelled like rotten jalapeño peppers. "I'm the one," he said, "who could kick the shit out of all three of you at once."

"Right, Joe," I said, hating myself. "Tragedy of Wisdom it is."

"Well, that sucked," I said.

"What sucked?" asked Rick.

Idiots Rule

Rick and I were on our way home after rehearsal in my clanking old gas-guzzling powder-blue Buick, which we had dubbed the Boat. I had bought the Boat off of a neighbor for four hundred dollars when I turned sixteen and crashed it a week later. But those old 1970s tanks were tough. With some coat hangers and duct tape to keep the headlights in place and the hood down, it worked just fine. It looked and sounded like a rolling scrap heap, but it still got me anywhere I wanted to go. That was important, because buses in Columbus, Ohio, were totally useless and my mom worked so much I could almost never count on her to give me a ride anywhere.

Rick lived down the street from me, so I always gave him a ride home after rehearsal. We'd known each other since kindergarten, and as much as we ragged on each other, we'd always been friends and we always would be.

"What do you mean, 'what sucked?'" I asked him. "Joe got his way. Again."

"It's not a big deal," said Rick. "You get too worked up about that kind of shit."

"It's the name of the band!" I said. "It's the first thing people are going to know about us, the first thing they're going to hear when we go onstage!"

"Who cares?" said Rick. "Look, you still get to play guitar. You still get to write all the songs. Joe isn't going to write them, that's for sure. He doesn't even know how to play an instrument. So let him have the stupid name. It'll probably be his only real contribution."

"Other than his singing," I said darkly.

"His grunting," corrected Rick.

"Like an ox in heat," I said.

"Hey, man," he said with a grin. "That's how they do it *hardcore*."

"Well," I said, "at least it's better than his first name suggestion."

"Yeah . . . what was it again?"

"Blubber Glove."

"Oh, right," said Rick. "Pretty much anything would be good compared to that."

Rick and I lived in German Village, a neighborhood just outside downtown that still had brick streets and narrow sidewalks like they did in the early 1900s. All the houses were old and small and packed in tightly together. It was pretty much the closest thing to urban you could get in a city like Columbus. It was getting kind of trendy, and my mom and I were probably the poorest people on our block, but it was where a lot of the creative types in town lived and there were lots of coffee shops and stores within walking distance. There wasn't really anywhere else in Columbus that I would've rather lived. Not like that's saying much. Columbus was pretty dull. Everyone who liked sports was really into OSU football, and pretty much everyone was into sports. Except freaks like me, I guess.

I dropped Rick off at his house, then drove home. We lived in a little brick townhouse. It was small, but it was enough for just me and my mom. It was dark and empty when I got inside because it was only seven and my mom worked until eight. I was supposed to start homework as soon as I got home, and honestly, even though there was no one around to enforce that rule, I considered it every night. But then it always felt like there wasn't any point. If I started early and finished early, my mom would just think I was slacking anyway. So it made more sense to do my own thing until she got home, and that way I'd have enough work to seem like an earnest, hardworking high school student.

I nuked a frozen dinner and took it up to my room. I busted out my guitar, a 1961 Gibson SG reissue that had taken me over a year to save up for (Mom paid one half for my birthday, and I paid the other). Then I sat down on the floor and got to work on the song I was writing. I sort of had a melody in my head. Nothing too complicated yet, but enough for me to get down some lyrics. It would be mainly drums and bass in the beginning, with just some guitar accents, real sharp and clean and quiet. I pulled out my notebook and stared for a moment at the title I'd written down: "Plastic Baby." I didn't know what it meant. It had just come bubbling out of my psyche or something during study hall. I tried to look at writing a song almost like solving a mystery. The song was there, buried somewhere in my brain. All I had to do was follow the clues until I figured it out. So I sort of hummed the backing sounds in my head and strummed lightly on my guitar until I had something more or less how I wanted it to sound, just quiet power chords mainly. Next I started humming the vocal melody while playing the guitar part. I did this a bunch of times until I didn't really need to think about it anymore and I could let my mind wander wherever. Then suddenly words just started coming:

Cain is dead forever.
Make believe forever.
Reason doesn't matter.
Tell you what I'm after.

Then I opened up with big, fat, loud open chords on the guitar, imagining in my head the ride cymbal on the drums coming into crashing, hissing life while I sang:

Idiots Rule

Plaaaaastiiiic baaaabeeee!

I had no idea what it meant yet. I usually didn't on a first verse and a chorus. But in the second verse you had to start getting more specific.

I'd been writing songs for a few years now. The early ones really sucked. Mostly they were just knockoffs of other songs. But the more I did it, the better I got. And having a band to write for made it all seem so much more real, so much more important. It wasn't just me doodling around anymore. These were songs that were going to get played.

I was in the groove now, so I kept going with the second verse. I played the first verse and chorus over and over again, trying to see how it would lead to the next verse. Sometimes it was that simple. But not this time. I kept playing, but nothing was coming. I started to get frustrated and strummed my guitar harder and harder. As awesome as it was to write songs for a band, it was tough, too. I had to always remember that it wasn't me who would be singing it. Not that I wanted to sing, of course. But when I wrote something, I'd sing it and it'd sound fine. My voice was kind of high, though, and when I'd bring it in for Joe to try with his gravelly, twenty-Camels-a-day voice, it just wouldn't sound right.

I tried the verse again, imagining him singing it instead of me. I even tried to mimic his voice, which was totally pathetic. And that just made me doubt myself more. So I got stuck and frustrated and I played so hard that I broke a string.

As I was restringing my guitar, the phone rang.

"Yeah?" I answered.

"Jen5 calling Samuel requesting a status report on Operation Rockstar."

"Hey, Fiver," I said.

Other than Rick, Jen5 was my best friend. There were four other Jennifers in our class. They quickly claimed "Jennifer," "Jenny," "Jen," and "J," so before someone could start calling her "Niffer" or "Furry," she let everyone know they could just call her Jen5. And whenever anyone asked her why, she'd say that it took five versions to get it perfect.

"Rehearsal was like eating a hot, steaming turd," I told her.

"Wow," she said. "Thanks for the visual."

"Joe started up on his bully routine and just *told* us that we were going to call the band Tragedy of Wisdom."

"That's so lame," she said. "Why don't you guys just tell him to get lost?"

"Ha," I said. "That's funny."

"Why? What's the worst that could happen?"

"He could murder us."

"He wouldn't do that."

"Wouldn't he? And anyway, we need a frontman. Someone with charisma."

"You have charisma," she said.

"No, I have a stupidity gene that possesses my mouth every time I should keep it shut."

"Whatever. You have way more charisma than Joe. That guy just yells a lot and looks scary. But you have genuine passion, you know? You're like a young Beethoven, all wild and crazy and totally committed to your music."

"Beethoven? You're such a nerd."

"Fine. As much as you secretly want me to, I'm not going to sit here all night and tell you how brilliant you are."

"Good," I said. "You're a terrible liar anyway."

"But you guys shouldn't have to put up with it. It can't be good for the band."

"No, it's fine," I said. "A ton of really great bands hate their lead singer. It's almost like a tradition, really. All the classic bands, like Jane's Addiction, the Pixies, Soul Coughing, had asshole lead singers."

"But none of those bands are around anymore, are they?"

"If we cut an album as sick as *Nothing's Shocking* or *Doolittle*, I'd be just fine with stopping after three or four," I said.

"Then what would you do with the rest of your life?"

"Huh?" I said. Then I heard the front door open and close. "Gotta go. My mom's home."

"Forget it." Jen5 sighed. "See you in art class."

"If you're lucky," I said.

"Ha," I heard her say just before I hung up.

Three, two, one . . .

"Samuel!" my mom yelled from downstairs. "Were you on the phone just now?"

"Yeah," I yelled back. The stupid phone downstairs lit up some big green light anytime someone was using it. I think she bought it just for that feature.

"Don't you have homework to do, young man?" she yelled up to me.

"I was asking Jen5 a history question." This was plausible. Jen5 was much better at history than I was. And better a half-truth, just in case she'd seen the caller ID.

"All I'm saying," she called, "is that I better not see any C's on the report card."

"Okay," I called back. "No C's."

D's and F's, maybe . . .

If she had come up to my room at that moment, I would have been completely screwed, because it would have been clear that I was doing just about everything *except* my homework. Guitar strings, my guitar, my songbook, and a pile of CD jewel cases all circled me like some kind of punk rock Stonehenge. But I knew she wouldn't check in for another half hour or so. My mom was a therapist, and I guess it was pretty rough having to listen to other people's problems all day, because when she came home she refused to do anything until she'd sat down and had a glass of white wine.

Still, I couldn't play my guitar and sing anymore, obviously. So I quietly restrung my guitar without tuning it, then cracked open my history books and began pretending to care.

"Sam?" Her voice was softer and thicker after a couple glasses of wine.

"Yeah, Mom?"

"Take a break from history for a minute," she said.

Like a dutiful son, I closed the textbook from which I had been reading the same paragraph over and over again because I just couldn't seem to pay attention to it.

"Talk to me," she said.

I turned away from my desk and looked at her.

For the most part, my mom was pretty cool. If she didn't understand me, it wasn't because she didn't try. My major complaint about my mom was that all of my friends, at some point, had to confess to me that they thought she was hot. Why couldn't they just keep it to themselves? Even Rick once said, "I mean, she's not my type or anything, but you have to admit, your mom is a total MILF!" I told him I would admit no such thing.

When we were first starting the band, Joe hadn't hooked up the Parks and Rec room yet. Rick, TJ, and I were hanging out one night, trying to think of places we could rehearse. TJ suggested my place. When I asked why, he said something about my mom maybe bringing us lemonade every once in a while. Well, I told him that one thing I was damn sure of, Joe would *never* meet my mom. TJ agreed that this was probably for the best.

"Hello?" my mom said. "Earth to Sam?"

"Sorry, Mom," I said.

"How was school?" she asked.

"Boring," I said.

"A few more details would be nice," she said.

"History is dumb. Spanish is hard. Math is pointless."

"What about English?"

"It's okay," I said. "We just finished *Beowulf,* which is about some knight dude, but they call him a Thane instead, and he kills this monster called Grendel, and then Grendel's mom gets upset and tries to kill him. So that's kind of interesting, I guess."

"What about science?"

"Science is just gross. We have to do these labs, right? Where we cut up plants and worms and stuff, and then we have to label all the parts on a worksheet."

"That sounds better than just reading things in books," said Mom.

"I guess," I said. Of course I couldn't tell her that at least I could fake reading things in textbooks. I didn't mind English or history, because they were about people. I felt like even Shakespeare had something to teach me about being a better songwriter. But science? Where was the poetry in cutting up slimy dead things?

"I know it's hard to see this right now, but science and math are really important. Colleges offer big scholarships for kids who excel at those subjects, and the variety of careers you can choose from is virtually endless."

"Mom, I'd rather gouge my eyes out with rusty spoons than study math. It's the lamest thing in existence. It's like the opposite of all creativity."

"Sammy, that's just not true. There's all sorts of amazing and wonderful things going on in math and science. Don't forget that it's going to be mathematicians and scientists who solve the world's ecology problems."

"Yeah, yeah."

"And computers. Video games. These things are made by math and science people."

"I know, I know. But it's still just numbers. And I'm not good at that stuff."

"You don't know that. You've never really even tried."

"Trust me, Mom. I'm not."

There was a moment of silence, during which I could tell I'd said something over the line, though I really couldn't see any flaw in my logic.

"Well," she said. "How was rehearsal?"

"Okay, I guess," I said.

"Okay, you guess?" she said.

"We're going to call ourselves Tragedy of Wisdom."

"Oh," she said. "That's nice."

See? Even she knew it was lame.

"Do you have rehearsal tomorrow after school?"

"No," I said. "TJ can't make it and Joe thinks that there's no point rehearsing without the drummer."

"Joe thinks," she said, rolling her eyes.

"What?" I said.

"Never mind," she said. "If you don't have too much homework tomorrow, could you spend a little time with your grandfather after school? He's been pretty down lately."

"Yeah, sure, I guess."

"You know it always cheers him up to see you."

"Sure doesn't seem like it," I said.

It takes me a long time to fall asleep. I'm not sure why. I don't really get tired like I guess a lot of people do. I mean, I wake up tired and stupid and slow, then as the day goes on, I get more and more awake until, by the time I'm supposed to go to bed, I'm totally wired. No, I don't eat a lot of sugar and I don't drink tons of soda or coffee. It's just how I am.

You know that buzzing sound you hear from old fluorescent lights? Not real obvious at first, but it kind of creeps up on you and gets really annoying after a while? Well, that's what runs through my head every night. So I just lay in bed in the dark and stare up at the ceiling while I wait for the buzzing to fade out. It always does, but sometimes it takes hours. And I can't close my eyes or I start to lose perspective on how big the room is and where I am in it, almost like I'm floating or sinking, and the buzzing gets so intense it feels like I'll drown in it. I used to read or listen to music in bed, but that only made things worse because not only would I have all my old thoughts from the day to settle down, but I'd be getting new ones also. So now I just stare up at the ceiling and wait.

The thing that kept floating through my head was Jen5's question: *What would you do with the rest of your life?*

But of course, I already knew the answer to that question. I'd just make more music. Despite its name, Tragedy of Wisdom was going to become famous. Not lame famous, like those sellout bands that play in football stadiums and can't even relate to regular people anymore. No, we were going to be cool famous, like those bands that hardly get any radio play, except on college radio, and if they have a video, it's only played late at night because it isn't commercial enough for the soulless marketing people. We were going to have one of those small but intense fan bases that would swap bootlegs of our shows online but buy the CDs anyway and totally obsess over my lyrics and what they meant. Cool writers would make references to us in their novels. Hot artsy chicks with nose rings would stalk us at concerts. The works.

That's what I planned to do with the rest of my life. Not bad, huh?

Communist Daughter

2

"I know what you're thinking," said Mr. Sully, our art teacher. "Fruit is soooo dullsville." He was an older guy with a long beard and long hair pulled back into a ponytail. Or at least, the hair he *had* was long. He was mostly bald on top. He looked more like he should be guarding a pot farm with a couple of Rottweilers down in southern Ohio than teaching art in a high school. But he was nice enough and kind of funny—at least, when he didn't mean to be.

"But I want tell you," continued Mr. Sully, nodding his head up and down rhythmically, "that painting a fruit still life can be awesome if you approach it the right way."

We were all standing in a big circle facing inward, each with an easel. In the center of the circle was an apple, a banana, and an orange on a table.

"I want you to think back to last year," said Mr. Sully, "and just muse on all the different styles of painting we talked about. I want you to meditate on them until you pick the one that speaks to you." He lowered his head, as if to show the proper posture for meditating, then he jerked his head back up, blinked, and said, "Then I want you to paint in that style. Okay. Begin."

"Fruit," said Jen5. "I hate painting fruit." Today she was decked out in a gray tweed sports coat over a black lacy tank top and torn-up flared jeans. Her massive tangle of frizzy, nearly dreadlocked blond hair was pulled back in some kind of leather-thong-and-chopstick combo.

Jen5 didn't really have a specific look or style. You couldn't pin her into a group like goth or geek or punk. Sometimes she looked like an art chick, sometimes like a skater chick, sometimes even a little like a college professor. But most of the time she looked like all three at once. The first thing that people noticed about her was the color of her eyes. Just like her style, you couldn't really tell what they were. Sometimes they were blue, sometimes green, sometimes gray or hazel. On official forms where you had to fill in stuff like your height, weight, and hair color, in the eye-color line she usually wrote "paisley."

"Fruit, flowers, sunsets," I said with a shrug. "What's the difference? It's all painting."

Jen5 scowled at me. "Sure, for you. Because you don't like painting. If you did, you'd know that there was a huge difference." Then she turned her scowl on the fruit. "Maybe if it was organic fruit or something . . . then it would have shades and variations. Stuff you could play with. But the stupid Frankenfruit they pump full of chemicals now, combined with all the wax they pour on it . . . we might as well be painting fake plastic fruit. There's nothing real about that. Nothing alive." Then she sighed, squirted some paint onto her palette, and went to town.

Visual art was definitely Jen5's thing. Drawing, painting, sculpture, photography, you name it. She kicked ass at all of it. It was amazing to watch how she attacked the canvas like she was pounding the colors into it. Paint flew everywhere—in her hair, on her clothes, smeared across her hands and face. It wasn't so much that she didn't care. It seemed more that she actually liked when it got messy. But as much as the paint was all over the place *off* the canvas, the paint *on* the canvas went exactly where she wanted.

"Wow, Jenny! Fantastic!" said Mr. Sully as he gazed at her half-finished painting. "I am totally feeling what you are putting down! Impressionistic fruit! Right on!"

Jen5 grunted without looking at him and continued painting, but I saw a little smile on her lips. She'd never admit it, but Mr. Sully was probably the only teacher whose opinion she valued.

Then Mr. Sully looked at my sad little picture. The only difference between the apple and the orange was the color. And the banana looked more like a wilted, yellow green bean.

"Ah." He nodded and patted me on the shoulder sympathetically. "Well, you just keep at it, Sam. I know you have the fire. This just isn't your medium, man."

"No kidding," I said.

"But that doesn't matter, you know," he said, his eyes getting dreamy. "All art, all creativity comes from the same place. Painting, music, dancing. It all comes from the same well. We drink and we are full. Are you feeling me?" he looked at me expectantly.

"Sure," I said. "Sure, Mr. Sully."

He nodded happily. "Just keep at it! Follow your bliss!" Then he floated off to babble at some other student.

"Wow, Sammy," said Jen5, looking over my shoulder at my painting. "That sucks."

"Eat me, Niffer," I said.

"Hey, I'm sure you'd say the same thing if you ever heard me try to sing."

"I've heard you sing," I said.

"What? When?"

"Third grade. School play. I believe the piece was entitled 'Peanut Butter and Jelly.' I was spellbound."

"I'm even worse now," she said, then turned and attacked her canvas again.

I just watched her paint for a little bit, then I said, "I think my mom doesn't want me to be a professional musician."

"Imagine that," she said, not looking away from her canvas.

"What do you mean?"

"When I told my mom I wanted to be an artist, do you know what she said? 'Oh, I'll love you even if you work at 7-Eleven your whole life.'"

"No she didn't."

"You better believe it."

"What does that even mean?" I asked. "That she thinks you'll never make it as an artist?"

"What she's really saying is that, in her book, being a successful artist is right up there with being a success at selling cigarettes to old ladies."

"Honestly, Fiver. Does she even get how bad that sounds?"

"Are you kidding? That's just her trying to be *funny*. If she actually thought I was serious, instead of just going through some teenage phase, she'd probably take away all my art supplies and ship me off to boarding school." She continued to dance around the easel, raking raw colors across the canvas. "As far as she's concerned, I'm on my way to a brilliant career as a doctor or lawyer."

"Yeah, that's totally ridiculous," I said. "But for your parents, in a weird parent kind of way, it makes sense. I mean, your mom *is* a lawyer. So of course that's what she wants you to be. But my grandfather was a professional musician. It was good enough for him, right? Why can't I be one too? I mean, most people our age don't even know what they want to do with themselves and they don't really care. But *I* care. I really want to be a musician."

Jen5 didn't say anything, but her brush started hitting the canvas hard enough for me to hear it.

"What?" I said.

She stopped painting and looked at me. "Do you think they really care about what we want, Sammy? Do you *really*?"

"Hey Sammy, I figured out how to play 'Peter Gunn'!" said Alexander.

Rick, TJ, and I had been friends a long time before the band got started. The other guy in our group was Alexander. He was brainiac smart and really good at soccer, but he didn't hang out with either the nerds or the jocks. Maybe it was because he was one of the few black kids in our school.

Maybe it was because he was also a skater and had worn oversized clothes for so many years that he didn't even know what his normal size was, and he had the biggest and most perfectly shaped fro that I'd ever seen. None of that fit in too well in central Ohio. But it was more than that. He was like a walking, talking They Might Be Giants song. He was always cheerful, always goofy, and just so *weird* that most of the time nobody understood what he was talking about. He was kind of like the weirdness mascot for our freaky little crew.

"What's 'Peter Gunn'?" asked Rick. We were all sitting around our lunch table. Rick looked even more out of it than usual. He had dark circles under his eyes, he looked like he hadn't showered, and he was slumped so far over the table that it made you feel like he needed it to keep from falling off the bench.

"You know," I said. "'Peter Gunn' was that Spy Hunter theme from the old-school Nintendo."

"Oh." Rick nodded. "I didn't realize it had another name."

"I think it was the theme song for a TV show in the fifties," said TJ.

"Huh," said Rick. "Was the Mario Brothers theme from something else too?"

"I don't think so," said TJ.

"Surprising," said Rick. "It was a catchy tune."

"What do you mean you figured out how to play it?" I asked Alexander.

"With my hands!" said Alexander.

All three of us groaned.

Alexander had really sweaty palms. Now, this was gross enough all by itself, but Alexander, in typical Alexander fashion, made it even worse when he figured out that by squeezing his sweaty palms together, he could get them to make a farting noise. Most meathead jocks would have laughed and maybe done it in Ms. Jansen's English class once or twice, then left it at that. But not Alexander. He didn't really even think it was funny. He thought it was *interesting*. So he kept experimenting with it until he realized that by applying different kinds of pressure, he could produce different tones. Since then, he had been attempting to play a song with hand farts.

"Wanna hear?" he asked now, his hands poised and his face eager.

"Not really," I said. But I knew it wouldn't do any good.

"Here goes!" he said, and began. His face screwed up in concentration as he worked his hands together, and sure enough, slowly we started to hear wet, squeaky notes: *phfip-phop phfip-phop phfip-phop phfffip-phfip!*

"Wow," said TJ. But he couldn't help grinning a little bit.

Alexander was getting warmed up now and the song was building momentum. It really did sound like "Peter Gunn." All three of us were nodding our heads in time, and Rick and I couldn't resist coming in with the second part over top:

"Baaaaa bah! Baaaaaaaaaa beeebah! Buh-buh-buh bah bah bah bah bah bah bah bah boo-buh-du!" We busted up laughing as Alexander continued to happily squeak away with his hand farts.

Then a velvety female voice cut through and said, "Hey, Sammy."

Silence. The speaker was standing directly behind me. I could see TJ and Alexander across from me with faces like deer in headlights. But I didn't need their expression to clue me in to who it was. Oh, God. I couldn't believe that *she'd* just witnessed our stupid freaky spectacle. I wanted to curl up like a pill bug and hide until graduation.

"Hi, Laurie," I said, trying to sound tough but only managing to sound hoarse. Then I turned around to look up at her.

Laurie was the hottest girl in school. She had straight, glossy black hair that hung to her shoulders; pale white skin; deep, mysterious green eyes; and full, pouty lips that were always covered in a dark burgundy lipstick. Today she was wearing a halter top, jean skirt, black fishnets (with a few artful rips), and knee-high black patent leather boots. In short, she was a goth goddess. And I was totally, helplessly in love with her.

My throat dried up as I tried to think of some way of explaining what we had just been doing that didn't make it sound even worse than it looked. All I could come up with was "How are you?"

"Okay." She smiled ever so faintly, but it was enough to send shivers down my spine. "Have you seen Joe today?"

My heart flopped down around my knees. Rick, who had listened to my miserable sighs and heartache for over a year now, choked on his soda.

"No," I said in a way that I hoped didn't sound as sad and desperate as I felt. "I think he skipped again today."

She sighed and bit her lip. "You guys have rehearsal tonight?"

"Uh, no," I said.

"Oh," she said. "Okay." She shifted her weight uncomfortably, then said, "Well, if you see him, tell him to call me."

"Sure," I said and valiantly attempted a smile. "Sure I will, Laurie."

"Thanks, Sammy." She gave another faint smile and then hurried off to sit with her girlfriends.

Our table seemed to breathe a collective sigh of relief.

"Dude," said Rick, giving me his most serious look. "Why didn't you invite her to sit with us?"

"Why would I do that?" I said.

He shrugged. "Hey, she's totally not my type, but I have to admit she's smoking hot. And anyway, you've been mooning over her our entire high school lives."

"Really?" asked TJ. "You have a thing for Laurie?"

"Never mind," I said. "It's just lame and depressing to talk about. And anyway, she's clearly not into me, so just let it go."

But *I* was the one who couldn't let it go.

"Why Joe?" I demanded. "What's he got that I don't?"

"He's older," said TJ.

"He's tougher," said Rick.

"He's the frontman," said Alexander. "Don't they always get the hot chicks?"

"Thanks, guys," I said. "Consider my ego boosted."

Then Jen5 flopped down next to me, spilling books and notebooks from her army bag in a cascade across the table. "What did Vampirella want?" she asked.

"She was asking where Joe was," said Rick.

"Ha," she said around a bite of salami sandwich. "Aren't they a match made in heaven."

"That's not what Sammy thinks," said Alexander.

"That's 'cause Sammy's a retard," said Jen5 without looking at me.

"I don't know why you don't like Laurie," I said. "I don't think you've really given her a chance."

"Oh, I gave her a chance all right. Back in junior high, before she'd discovered goth and was just another snobby prep girl. We were supposed to sell Girl Scout cookies together and—"

"You were in the Girl Scouts?" asked Alexander.

"For one year," I said.

"My parents were concerned about my antisocial behavior," Jen5 said with a shrug. "They thought it would bring me out of my shell. But as the case with Miss Vampirella illustrates, a year of merit badges, cookie sales, car washes, and memorized slogans may have made me more social, but it didn't do much good for the 'anti' part."

"So what happened?" said Rick. "Did you slap her or something? Pull her hair out?"

"Grow up," she said.

"Never!"

"Anyway, we were supposed to sell cookies together, and I was trying to talk to her like she was a normal human being and not some brainless Kewpie doll until finally she turned to me and said: 'Uh, hey, Jen. My friend's mom just pulled into the parking lot, so if you could just, like, not talk to me until she's inside the store and can't see us anymore, I'd really appreciate it.'"

"You are lying," I told Jen5.

"You wish," she said.

"You know what I heard about love?" TJ asked suddenly.

We all stared at him.

"Uh, no," I said, wondering where this came from. "What did you hear?"

"That everyone has an image in their mind of the perfect girl or guy. And whenever someone fits eighty percent of that image, we block out the rest. We just don't even see it. And we continue to block it out until we get to know them so well that we're comfortable with them. Then we finally see the other twenty percent and it could be the worst thing in the world and we just never noticed before."

"Well, by all means, then," said Jen5. "Let us hasten this connection between Laurie and Sammy so that he might see the idiocy of his desire more quickly! Hopefully he won't get crabs in the process!"

"Jesus, why do you have to be like that?" I said. "TJ's trying to talk about something serious and you can't even . . ."

She was just sitting there smirking at me. Maybe she was one of my best friends, but she also pissed me off a lot.

"You know what?" I said. "Just forget it." And I got up, grabbed my bag, and left the table.

As I walked away, I heard her call to me, "Come on now! Sammy! Don't be such a spaz! I was only kidding!"

But I knew she wasn't. Jen5 only smiled when she was dead serious.

After school, I pulled the Boat up in front of my grandfather's apartment building. He lived on the first floor of a place just outside German Village, so it didn't have to keep that old-building look. I cut the ignition and waited while the Boat's engine settled, listening to the groaning tick of the radiator slow down to silence. I was stalling. I didn't really want to see him. I mean, I did. I loved my grandfather, maybe more than anyone else, but . . . well . . . he was getting a little crazy in his old age. I was tempted to skip it completely and tell Mom he was asleep or something. But I knew I wouldn't do that. It'd make me miserable all night thinking about it. So after another five minutes of staring at my dashboard, I decided to face the music.

Literally.

When I stepped through the front door, noise hit me like a brick in the face. The lights were dim, and as I waited for my eyes to adjust, I tried to figure out what was in the noise. The

Oscar Peterson Trio. Billie Holiday. And something else more modern, probably Wynton Marsalis. Three totally different jazz artists being blasted from three different stereos at the same time. And there was something else that I couldn't figure out. It wasn't until my eyes finally adjusted to the gloom that I saw it was my grandfather playing the piano. That gave me a little hope, because these days he usually only played when he was in a good mood.

I walked through the living room and over to the piano, then stopped and watched him play for a minute.

He was mostly bald, and the little bit of white hair he had around the sides and back was frizzy, almost like cotton candy. He had a short beard, which I always thought was a good idea for an old guy. It covered up that turkey neck that most of them got. He looked skinnier every time I saw him. He had a nurse or aide or whatever they were called who came in and made him breakfast, but I don't think he could afford any more help than that, so the only other time he ate was when Mom or I came to visit and made something for him. Eating just didn't interest him very much anymore.

He didn't seem to notice me, or else he didn't feel like talking. He just kept playing. After a little while, I went into the kitchen. His freezer was filled with the same frozen dinners that filled ours. Mom just bought a ton of them at some warehouse club. I pulled out two and popped them in the microwave.

While I stared at the revolving plastic trays through the microwave door, I heard the Wynton Marsalis album finish. Right after the microwave timer dinged, the Oscar Peterson Trio stopped. While I was setting the tiny kitchen table for us, Billie Holiday stopped too. All that was left was my grandfather's piano. It was a little out of tune and it sounded like he couldn't quite make up his mind whether he was playing lounge or swing style. But I liked listening to him. It reminded me of when I was a kid and my mom used to take me to see him play. It hadn't happened a lot, because he usually played at nightclubs and other places my mom didn't think a kid should be. But every once in a while he'd have a gig at a regular concert hall, usually backing up some famous musician on tour. I'd also get to hear him when my mom was going to school at night to get her graduate degree. She'd drop me off at Gramps's place and we'd sit in front of the piano most of the night. He'd play lots of old big band tunes and teach me the words and I would sing along. He still lived in the same apartment, but it seemed brighter and warmer in my memory.

He was playing Duke Ellington's "I'm Beginning to See the Light." It was one of his favorites, so I knew it really well.

I began to sing along:

"I never cared much for moonlit skies. I never wink back at fireflies."

I tried to remember what he looked like back then. He used to wear lots of beatnik turtlenecks and berets and heavy sweaters. I remembered that. But I couldn't picture his face. I knew he used to smile a lot, but I couldn't remember what that looked like. A year ago he had to retire from playing because he was having trouble remembering songs, and he hadn't really been the same since.

"Boy, are you going to stare at that food or are you going to eat it?" said Gramps.

I'd been so zoned out that I hadn't noticed he'd stopped playing. Now he was standing in the kitchen doorway glaring at me.

"Hey, Gramps," I said. "Dinner's ready."

"I can see that!" he said, and sat down at the table. "I'm not completely blind, you know!"

"I know, Gramps."

"Just mostly."

"Yep."

"Haven't lost my perfect-pitch ear, though."

"Nope," I lied. "Have something to eat." I nudged his tray. He shook his head. "You first."

"Gramps," I said. "I swear I didn't put anything in it." My mom doesn't think he takes his medication regularly, so sometimes she tries to slip it into his food.

His eyes narrowed and he gave me a weird look, like he thought I might be lying. "How do I know for sure? Why don't you take a bite and prove it to me?"

I rolled my eyes to show him I thought he was being totally ridiculous, but I took a bite of his food and chewed slowly while he watched me carefully. I guess he was waiting to see if I keeled over and started foaming at the mouth or something. When he was sure none of that was going to happen, he sat down and started shoveling food in so fast I couldn't believe he had time to swallow.

"That damn McCarthy was here again today," he said between bites.

"Again?" I asked. He'd recently been talking about this guy a lot. Senator Joseph McCarthy was some freaky congressman in the '50s who went around trying to prove that artists, actors, and musicians were all communist spies for Russia. No matter what I said, Gramps refused to believe that the guy died in 1957. At first it had been weird the way he always went on about him, but after a while it got kind of fun. So now I played along with it.

"Do you think he's on to you?" I asked.

"Ha! I'm no commie, and certainly no spy." He stirred his beef stew around a little bit, then looked back at me fiercely. "I'm a socialist! But the distinction between a commie scum and a thoughtful socialist is far too difficult for an ignoramus like McCarthy to grasp."

I couldn't really figure out the difference either, but I still played along. "That's the truth," I said.

Gramps was getting more worked up now. "Last I checked, this was still a free country!"

"I don't think you have to worry about him, Gramps."

He placed his fork on the side of his nose and gave me a wink. "Damn right." When he took the fork away, there was a blob of gravy on the side of his nose. Then he frowned. "What about you?"

"Me?"

"Have you covered your tracks?" he asked, looking worried. "I can't have my own grandson in prison!"

"Gramps, I'm not a commie *or* a socialist."

"Ha! You think that matters to scum like McCarthy? He and his kind despise musicians. They can't comprehend living a life of creativity and individualism! They try to turn anything you do into some kind of anti-American statement."

"Really, Gramps," I said. "I don't think it's a problem."

He didn't look very convinced. Finally, he said, "Well, tell me what your set list is right now. That's usually where they start looking, to see what kind of songs you're playing."

I told him the set list we were working on.

"I don't recognize any of those songs," he said.

"That's because I wrote them."

"Wrote?" He blinked in confusion. "Why? Can't you play anyone else's songs?"

"Sure we could."

"Then why are you writing your own? Only people who can't play the standards have to make up their own songs."

"That's not how it is anymore, Gramps. Most people play their own music."

"That's ridiculous! Are you telling me that at your age, you're writing better songs than the Duke? Than Bird? I love you, kid, but somehow I think you've got a few more years before you're ready for that."

"Gramps, nowadays you only play other people's music if you can't write your own."

"An entire generation of arrogant hacks." He sighed. "Let me tell you something, kid. In all my years in clubs and bars, on cruise ships, and in festivals and concert halls, I was never forced to play anything that I had to *make up*."

"I know, Gramps," I said. There didn't seem to be much point in arguing with him. He wasn't even listening.

"So." Gramps gazed balefully down at me, his old eyes wide and a little wild. "When are you getting married?"

Like clockwork. Music and girls. The only things he could think about.

"Gramps," I said, "I'm only seventeen."

"SO WHAT? When I was your age I'd already met the love of my life. Your grandmother. Vivian . . ." He sighed and his eyes went unfocused. "You don't remember her, do you?"

"Not really," I said. "Although I think I remember her perfume, you know? I have this really vivid memory of sitting on someone's lap while I watched you play at some festival. And I know it wasn't Mom because of the way she smelled."

"God, I loved her," said Gramps, his eyes and voice drifting farther away until it was almost like he was talking to himself. "Viv. She was a real beauty. And kind, oh so kind. Your mother got her looks. Not too much of the kindness, though. Viv understood how hard it was to be a musician. She understood what a wretched, callous thing life can be to an artist. She was a singer herself, see. A voice like a fallen angel. And for a while, a short, sweet while, we were together, partners in crime, and we could handle *anything* . . ."

He was blinking away tears as he looked up at the ceiling. He really wasn't the crying type, so seeing him like that made me a little uncomfortable. Then, still looking up at the ceiling, his hand groped across the table until it found mine, and grasped it hard.

"Oh God, how I loved that woman," he whispered.

I patted the top of his hand, all liver spots and paper-thin skin, and said, "I know, Gramps. I know."

After that, I felt like I couldn't just leave after dinner. So I stayed pretty late and we talked about music and girls, like always. His mood swings kept me kind of off balance, the way he would be angry and ranting and then suddenly get all sad and teary. But he was in one of his poetic moods, so he talked on and on about Parker and Gillespie, Davis and Coltrane. Names that I had heard whispered throughout my life with absolute reverence. These were gods to him, and I loved hearing him talk about them and about their music. It wasn't just about his jazz. He would talk about how important *all* music was. How it took us—not just the people who played it but the people who heard it—to a place above the normal boring world. A place of pure beauty. And that would somehow always lead him into talking about beautiful women. And how they were the last refuge of the creative soul in this harsh, modern world.

Sure, he was moody and a little crazy. But how could you not love him?

Someday You Will Be Loved

3

Classes always seemed to go on forever when you had something cool planned at night. That day seemed endless because later I was going to see Monster Zero play.

I was actually a little nervous to see them. They had been playing in the local scene for a couple years and they had a big following. They'd even had a regional tour, up to Cleveland and Detroit, down to Cincinnati, west to Indianapolis, and east to Pittsburgh, to promote an album they'd made on a local indie label. If you were in the scene, you knew who they were. But it wasn't like you could buy their album in New York, L.A., or even Seattle. They were ours alone. That was until last week, when some cheesy mainstream rock magazine had named Columbus "The Next Seattle." During the grunge thing in the early '90s, major labels could pick up unknown bands in Seattle and make a ton of money off of them by calling it "alternative rock." Ever since, they'd been trying to do the same thing someplace else, getting their marketing minions to convince us that some up-and-coming city was the new cool scene. One year, the year Death Cab for Cutie got big, they even named Seattle "The Next Seattle." How dumb was that? I guess some people believed it—the ones who watched MTV and read stupid mainstream rock magazines. But anyone who was already in the scene knew it was total bullshit.

But now Columbus had been named the new "Next Seattle" and Monster Zero had been named the best band in the Columbus scene. Tonight was their first gig since the magazine article came out. Would they be the same cool band they'd always been? Or would the lure of money and national fame have already sunk its claws into them?

At last the final bell rang, and I went straight home. I had to change, eat dinner, call everybody to figure out who was driving who and where we would all meet up, and be out the door before Mom got home and officially reminded me it was a school night and gave me a curfew. I didn't like going against her directly, but if we didn't talk about it before I left, then I could be a little later that night and plead misunderstanding or forgetfulness. As long as I wasn't too ridiculously late, she'd let me slide.

Rick lived closest to me, so I picked him up first. When I turned on to his block, I saw him sitting out on the curb waiting for me. His house was much nicer than mine. His mom was a doctor and his dad was in finance (whatever that meant), so they made a lot of money. Although you wouldn't know it, looking at Rick. If anything, it looked like he'd tried to make himself look even scruffier since school let out. But that didn't mean he could resist taking shots at me.

"Boat's getting worse," he said as he climbed into the passenger seat.

"What do you mean?" I asked.

"I came outside as soon as I heard it coming, thinking it was only a block or two away, but I've been out here for ten minutes."

"Ha-ha," I said.

"Swear to God, I think I heard you turn the ignition."

"You wanna walk?"

"I'm just concerned for the health and well-being of our only mode of transport. Maybe you should take it to a shop or something. Have it looked at."

"You wanna pay for that?"

"My money's all tied up in investments." That was his usual joke response when people asked him for money. It's what his dad said when he'd asked why he couldn't have a car if they were so rich.

"Anyway," I said, "I'm sure they'd probably tell me to sell it for scrap or something. It's only my remarkable Zen powers that keep it moving."

"You, Sammy?" said Rick. "You're the anti-Zen."

"What does that mean?"

"Never mind. Let's go pick up the floozy and then see that sell-out band."

When we pulled up to Jen5's house, she wasn't waiting out front for us. That was normal, though, because her dad said it was rude if we didn't come inside and say hello to him. It was kind of like we had to ask his permission to take her out with us.

We parked the Boat out front, then trooped single file up the narrow, winding walkway through the little rose garden and up to the front door. There was no doorbell because, according to Jen5, the sound of doorbells didn't agree with her mother's nerves. Instead they had a big iron knocker that I guess did agree with her nerves. I picked it up and clanked it against the door a few times. We heard shouts from inside that sounded like Jen5 and her father. Her mother was probably still at work. She worked even more than my mom did. But her father, who was some kind of language professor at Ohio State University, was home all the time.

Rick and I knew better than to just open the door like we did at each other's houses, so we stood and waited until the shouting match was over. Then we heard several deadbolts unlock and a chain slide, and the big heavy door creaked open.

On the other side of the door, Jen5's father glared down at us. He was really good at glaring, probably because he had to do it a lot with his students. And he wasn't one of those flustered, stuffy, egghead-type professors. He was more like some old English lord, except dressed in preppy clothes that Jen5's mother had probably picked out. He was tall and really thin, and he had these intense, piercing eyes that didn't miss a thing.

"Good evening, Mr. Russell," said Rick. "We'd like to kidnap your daughter and sell her to the gypsies. We'll give you twenty percent off the top."

Unless it was humor. Mr. Russell *never* got humor. He continued to glare down at us, but one of his bushy white eyebrows twitched a little.

"Gentlemen," he said. "Come in, please." As we walked dutifully into the foyer, he called up the staircase, "Jennifer, your friends have arrived."

"Where are my pants?" she called down from somewhere upstairs.

"Which pants?" he called back up.

"The ones you hid from me because you said they looked like they were owned by a bum."

"Homeless person," he corrected her. Then, "I threw the pants away."

"Liar," she yelled down. "You never throw away anything."

He paused for a second, his face totally expressionless. Then he said, "You might find them in the attic, then. In your keepsake chest."

"In my . . . ," she began, but her voice trailed away as we heard her stomp up a second flight of stairs.

Mr. Russell turned back to us, still completely dignified.

"Jennifer will be down momentarily."

We stood there for a little bit, all three of us uncomfortable. But Rick couldn't take all the seriousness, so he said, "Say, Mr. Russell. Your rose bushes are looking splendid."

Mr. Russell glared down at Rick, but Rick held on to his earnest expression of innocence.

"Thank you, Richard," said Mr. Russell.

Then Jen5 came down the steps, skipping half of them on her way.

"Let's get out of here," she said.

"When will you be home, dear?" asked Mr. Russell.

"Before Mom is," said Jen5.

"Ah," said Mr. Russell. Then he turned to me. "Samuel, I trust you will have my daughter home at a reasonable hour."

"Sure thing, Mr. Russell," I said. I couldn't bring myself to make fun of him like Rick did. There was just something kind of sad about him. I imagined him sitting in the big stuffed chair he had in his study, drinking tea or sherry or something, reading depressing poetry for hours and hours while he waited for his family to get home. I don't know. I just can't be mean to someone like that.

As soon as we were outside and the door was shut behind us, Rick called, "Shotgun!"

"Chivalry," said Jen5, "is so dead."

Monster Zero was playing at a local venue just off the OSU campus called Saul's Subs. It was supposed to be a deli, and they did serve sandwiches and stuff, but there was also a bar attached called the Brewery. Since they were technically two places that just happened to share a wall, they could do all-ages shows. That combo made it popular for both high school kids and college kids, so it was usually pretty hopping. In fact, it was probably the best venue in town for local bands. It usually had just the right amount of space.

But not tonight. I guess the hype from the stupid music magazine had brought in a lot of people who didn't usually see local bands, so the place was completely mobbed. Rick, Jen5, and I pushed our way through the crowds of sweaty jock and cheerleader types who normally wouldn't be caught dead in a place like this. I felt like we had been invaded and the place didn't have its usual cool vibe at all. Instead, it felt weirdly tense, like a school dance, with lots of people sizing each other up.

"This sucks," I told Jen5.

She shrugged. "Price of fame, I guess."

"Fame sucks," I said.

"You'll keep saying that right up to the point when you're discovered by a record label."

"Let's find a place in the back to hang out," Rick yelled over the noise.

"We have to find TJ first," I said. "He's here by himself."

Rick looked around at the mass of shoulder-to-shoulder people. "That won't be fun," he said. "Why can't TJ find us?"

"Jesus, Rick," said Jen5. "Come on, let's at least try to look around a little."

We made our way through the crowds, scanning the top for TJ's mop of brown hair. While we were looking, I spotted Joe and Laurie in a dark corner making out. Rick followed my look.

"Shit!" he said.

"Come on, guys," said Jen5, pushing us on.

"Did you see that, Fiver?" asked Rick. "Joe's totally grabbing her tit."

"Yeah, yeah," she said. "Keep it moving."

We found TJ backed up against a wall looking lost and bewildered. Like he couldn't even comprehend all the trendy people swarming around him. The look of relief in his eyes when he saw me wave to him made me feel like I'd just thrown him a life preserver. But by the time we worked our way over to him, we didn't really have any time to talk because Monster Zero was onstage.

Nobody noticed right away. The band just climbed up there, all casual, like they couldn't care less that this was the biggest crowd they'd ever played to. It wasn't until they started tuning up that people noticed and started to get quiet.

Eric Strom, the lead singer, looked more like a computer geek than a rock star. He had thick, square glasses and short spiky hair, and he always wore thin polyester button-up shirts.

He waited until the crowd was looking at him, then he cleared his throat.

"Wow," he said into the mic, totally chill. "Listen, I just have one thing to say to you people: Don't believe everything you read."

And then the band blasted into their first song. A wall of noise washed over the crowd, punctuated by Eric's howling vocals. Somehow, in a split second, he'd transformed before our eyes into a punk rock god. This was charisma. This was what I was talking about when people asked me why I wasn't the lead singer. Because I didn't have that.

Eric's energy, backed by the sheer power of the band, transported me, and suddenly the crowds didn't matter. Joe and Laurie groping each other didn't matter. An army of marketing minions and their bullshit magazines didn't matter. There was just this band doing their thing.

It's hard to explain. When I'm playing music, that's when I feel most alive. I escape from all the crap: no doubts, no worries, no fears. Just me. And when I listen to really good music, especially if it's live, it's the same thing. I'm transported and nothing else matters.

When Monster Zero finished their set, I came back to the real world and looked around. Half the people had left at some point. I hadn't noticed, and I didn't really care. Because I knew that Monster Zero was for real. They wouldn't sell out. They had proved that to me. And I was so relieved. I almost felt like crying. Not cool, I admit. But at the same time, I didn't want that feeling to ever end.

"Sam," said Jen5. "It's time to go home."

"Yeah," I said, and all the fears and doubts that I had escaped came flooding back, making me feel twenty pounds heavier. "I guess you're right."

"That'll be you someday," said Jen5.

"Most of the time I think so," I said. "But when I see a *real* band play, as much as I love it, it makes me feel like we've still got a long way to go."

"You *are* a real band, Sammy."

"We've only performed twice, and we didn't finish our set either time."

"Well, okay . . . ," she said. "It wasn't your fault some neighbor called the cops on Laurie's birthday party. You guys weren't really playing that loud. That neighborhood is just full of old rich snobs who hate teenagers. And getting shut down by the cops is kind of cool, right?"

"What about the show in Heath?" I asked.

"Was that the one you did at the Union Hall with a couple of other bands that Joe knew?"

"Hey," said Rick, breaking into the conversation. "Are you

guys taking about that gig we did where all those rednecks were heckling us?"

"Yeah," I said. "It didn't help that Joe decided to do an impromptu version of that old Camper Van Beethoven song."

"'Take the Skinheads Bowling,' right?" He laughed a little. "That was pretty funny, you have to admit."

"Right up until they rushed the stage and nearly beat the shit out of us."

"We got away, didn't we?" asked Rick.

"The point is, we've never had a real gig," I said. "One that went well."

"Just believe in yourself," said Jen5. "Don't give up."

I smirked at her. "Thanks for the pep talk, Coach."

She rolled her eyes. "Fine. You're going to work at 7-Eleven your whole life. Happy now?"

Wake Up

4

The next morning, I stood in the hallway at school and stared at a new poster for a long time. Somewhere in the back of my mind I was thinking that the bell had rung and I was going to be late for class. But still I looked at the poster.

It was glossy black with that messy "thrasher" font that had been designed to appeal to teenagers like me. The poster said:

THINK YOUR BAND ROCKS?
PROVE IT!

KLMN 103.1 FM IS SPONSORING A BATTLE OF THE
BANDS ON OCTOBER 1ST, AT THE NEWPORT MUSIC HALL.
GRAND PRIZE IS FREE STUDIO TIME TO RECORD A

SINGLE THAT WILL BE PLAYED
BY KLMN DURING A PRIME-TIME SLOT!
SO WHAT ARE YOU WAITING FOR?
FAME AND FORTUNE START HERE WITH

KLMN 103.1 FM!
YOU HAVE PERMISSION TO ROCK!

I couldn't stop staring at the poster. It amazed me that the people who came up with this garbage thought they could get to us with this kind of stuff. A Battle of the Bands? How utterly lame. Music wasn't a competition like football. Not that I expected a poser radio station like KLMN to get that. On the other hand, free studio time to lay down a professional-sounding track . . . that sounded really nice. And how funny would that be to have one of our songs playing on KLMN? And maybe then Mom would lay off about the math and science stuff.

But who was I kidding? A station like that wouldn't even like our sound. And anyway, I wasn't sure we were ready for a big venue like that yet. But I still couldn't stop staring at the poster.

"That's right, Sammy," said a low, gruff voice behind me.

Joe.

"We're going to enter this poser contest," he said. "And we're going to kick all their asses and get a single on that wannabe radio station. And then they will all understand what real hardcore is about."

The way he said it was so totally confident. Like there was no other way it could go.

"Seriously?" I asked. "You want to join a Battle of the Bands?"

"Why the hell not?" said Joe.

I looked up at him, into his hard, angry eyes and his perpetual sneer, and it made me feel better. Yeah, I thought. Why not? What did we have to lose? Sometimes it was really good to have Joe on your side.

"Joseph McConnahay and Samuel Bojar!"

We both turned and saw Ms. Jansen's head sticking out of her classroom door. She glared at us from behind her thick octagonal glasses. "Gentlemen, are you waiting for an invitation?"

"Ah, Ms. Jansen," said Joe, stretching his arms out wide. "I was just trying to peel young Samuel's eyeballs off of this Battle of the Bands poster." He started walking over to her in a casual swagger. "He seems to think that rock and roll is more important than literature. Can you believe it? The next thing you know, he'll be sacrificing goats to Lord Satan!"

"That's not funny, Joseph," said Ms. Jansen.

"My humble apologies," said Joe with a wicked grin. He had told us many times that he had a way with older women, but I could never tell if teachers like Ms. Jansen were really charmed by his little act or if they only tolerated it because, deep down, they were just as scared of him as we were.

"Just get in here," was all she said.

At lunch, I didn't go to our usual table. Even though Joe sounded completely confident that we would win the Battle of the Bands, I still wasn't sure about it. So I found a little cubby under a staircase and quietly chewed my sandwich and worried.

"Hiding?"

I looked up and saw Jen5 peeking into my cubby.

"Nah," I said. "Meditating."

"Great," she said. "Mind if I sit with you?"

"Well, it'll delay my quest for enlightenment, but I guess that's one of the trials I must face if I am to become the next Dalai Lama."

"Oh, good," she said and plunked down next to me. "'Cause I need help with English."

"Oh, yeah?" I said.

"Yeah. *Macbeth*. Help me."

Wake Up

"With what?"

"What's it about?"

"Didn't you read it?"

"Of course I did. But they're always going off on these tangents about gods and stuff. I keep losing track of the story."

"Well, you know we were only supposed to read the first act for today, but it's actually a pretty intense story, so I just did the whole thing," I said. "I'm kind of amazed that Ms. Jansen was allowed to assign it to us, because it's crazy violent."

"Really?" said Jen5 as she pulled out her salami sandwich. "What did I miss?"

"Okay, well, Macbeth is this thane, right? This knight-warrior dude. And he's won all kinds of battles for his king. But then he runs into these creepy witches who can see the future, and they tell him he'll be king someday. And that totally obsesses him. He wants all that power, right? So he tells his wife about it and she's like, 'Let's not wait around for this to happen. Let's *make* it happen. Like, tonight.' So they kill the king and Macbeth takes over and then he just turns into this total power-hungry psycho. Just goes around killing people, even friends and little kids and stuff."

"He kills kids?" she asked, the sandwich halfway to her mouth.

"Totally. Lots of them. And the witches give him all these

weird riddles, like 'Nobody can kill you except someone who wasn't born from a woman.' And he's like, 'Awesome. Everybody's born from a woman, so I'm totally safe.' But then this dude named Macduff shows up who technically wasn't *born* from a woman. He was ripped out of her womb."

"Gross!" said Jen5.

"Yeah, then Macduff kills Macbeth, chops his head off, and sticks it on the wall of the castle."

"And that's the end of the story?"

"That's it."

"Wow," said Jen5. Then she finally took a bite of her salami sandwich. She frowned at it and shoved it back into her bag. "You know, I think I might become a vegetarian."

"Why's that?" I asked. "Feel bad about killing animals, or just want to be trendy?"

"I'm serious. Some days, meat just seems gross to me. Like I can't believe we put stuff like that into our bodies. Especially right after hearing you talk about babies being ripped from their mothers' wombs."

I shrugged and took a big bite of my roast beef.

"I wouldn't want to be a vegan, though," she said. "I like cheese too much."

"And leather boots," I said, nudging the cowboy boots she was wearing with her plaid pants—a look that somehow made sense on her. "Vegans don't wear leather, I think. No animal products of any kind."

"Yeah, screw that," she said.

We both stared at her boots for a minute. Then she said, "So why are you hiding down here?"

"I'm not hiding," I said.

"You know what I mean."

"There's some Battle of the Bands that KLMN is hosting," I said, "and Joe wants us to enter."

"So?"

"So, I don't know if we should do it."

"Why not?"

"Well, I mean, come on. A Battle of the Bands? That's totally lame."

"Why?"

"They're just so . . . commercial, you know?"

"So? Do you get anything if you win?"

"Free studio time and radio play."

"Well, that's pretty sweet."

"Yeah, I know . . ."

"Listen, you don't have to sell your soul or anything, right? They aren't making you change your songs or anything."

"Yeah, but—"

"So, you use the system. You make it happen *your* way."

"I guess, but—"

"What?"

"Well, I don't know if we're ready," I admitted.

"Don't you have enough songs written?"

"We have enough songs."

"So what's the problem?" she asked, starting to get a little annoyed.

"I just . . . don't think we sound very good. Yet."

"Oh."

"Yeah," I said. "I mean, I know we'll be amazing once we get it all together. But right now, Rick is always mixing up bass lines. Playing the wrong one. And it doesn't seem like he notices."

"Or cares," muttered Jen5.

"And then, Joe—"

"Can't sing a note."

"That doesn't really matter," I said. "But the problem is we've been playing for months now and he doesn't know the words to any of the songs yet. Both times we've played in front of an audience, he had to have little typed pieces of paper. And you can't do something like that at a big, radio-sponsored event."

"Hmm," said Jen5. "And when's this thing happening?"

"Two weeks."

"Yikes."

Wake Up

"Yeah. We just better start practicing a little more often, is all. Like daily. Starting today."

Fortunately, Rick, TJ, and I had computer lab that afternoon. C Lab was one of those pathetic no-brainer classes where as long as you showed up, you got an A, probably because most of the students already knew more about computers than the teacher. It was only the stubborn pride of the educators who, unwilling to admit that they could take some pointers from us, set up a curriculum that only required us to be able to edit a Word doc and send an e-mail in order to pass. And the best part was that while they had blocked instant messaging and a lot of specific "bad" sites, like MySpace, they hadn't even considered message boards. So Rick, TJ, and I would find some dead or near-dead board and post back and forth for the entire class.

Modboy: where were you @ lunch, sam?

Samlam: thnkign spot. u gents see the klmn poster?

Rickosity: yup

Samlam: cool?

Modboy: u bet!

Samlam: we better practice . . . tnight?

Modboy: Joe stopped me in the hall, said he couldn't do tonight

Samlam: WTF!!! Y?!

Modboy: didn't say

Samlam: ARGHHHH!

Rickosity: o good . . . wuz worried i'd be the one to cancel

Modboy: you? why?

Rickosity: got the new pfect drk last night

Samlam: u would cancel for that?

Modboy: Halo3, maybe, but Perfect Dark?

Rickosity: d0ods, you ain't played it yet

Modboy: good?

Rickosity: brilliant

Samlam: you guyz are nerds!

Rickosity: its fri, the rents are AWOL and you guys are coming for a night of beer -n games!

Samlam: well . . . if we can't rehaerse . . .

Rickosity: thats the spirit!

Modboy: invite Alex?

Rickosity: done, son

Samlam: good. he's the only one who can beat u

Rickosity: cant just laugh at u losers . . . BTW, invite Jen5?

Samlam: she hates games but she DOES like beer

Rickosity: thats 4 sure

Modboy: 2 much?

Rickosity: 2 much is never enough

Samlam: sez alky

Rickosity: yer jealous yer mom dont buy u brew

Modboy: if I was sammy, i wouldn't be jealous of

ANYBODY ELSES MOM!

Samlam: you suck. we'll settle this tonight on xbox!

Modboy: bring it

After knocking back a few beers and murdering each other a dozen times, we decided that the latest Perfect Dark, though good, was still no Halo, so we switched over. There was a whole lot of trash talk floating through the air, mainly from Rick and Alexander because, as usual, TJ and I were getting our asses kicked.

Rick tossed his controller aside, yelled, "More beer for the victor!" and stalked into the kitchen area. Rick's house was completely open downstairs, so there weren't really any separate rooms. His mom was an interior decorator and their house always felt a little like a showroom.

"So where's Five?" asked TJ.

"She said she'd stop by at some point," I said.

"But you never know with her," said Rick from the kitchen. "Best thing to do is assume she isn't coming. Then you might be pleasantly surprised."

"Don't you like her?" said TJ.

"Fiver?" asked Rick as he came back and handed beers around. "She's awesome. She's just weird."

"How so?" asked TJ.

"Boy," said Rick, nudging Alexander, "you get a few into TJ and he can't stop talking about Fiver."

Alexander had started up a solo game of Halo, and he looked completely zoned into it, but he spoke in a way that sounded almost rehearsed. "I noticed that too, Richard. What do you think it means?"

"Well, young Alexander, some guys get stuck on a girl, you know?"

"Hey, wait a minute . . . ," said TJ.

"Hmmm . . . ," said Alexander. "Richard, I'm not sure I know what you mean. Perhaps you could explain further."

"It's simple, Alexander," said Rick. "Sometimes, when a man sees a woman who is eighty percent like his ideal mate, his judgment becomes cloudy and his heart begins to pound."

"Wait," I said. "You don't mean . . ."

Rick gave me a wicked grin. "Oh, yeah. TJ's got a big old crush on the Fiver!"

Rick and Alexander thought this was hilarious for some reason. I guess I was supposed to think so too, because Rick kept looking over at me with this weird grin.

TJ was blushing bright red now as he glared at Rick and Alexander. "Why are you guys laughing? I mean, what's wrong with it?"

"Nothing," said Rick, and then laughed again.

"I mean," said TJ, "she's cool, right? And pretty hot?"

"Yeah, sure." Rick shrugged. "She's not my type or anything, but in her own funky way, she's smokin'."

TJ's face was still red, but I realized it was probably just as much anger as embarrassment. "You're always saying that so-and-so isn't your type. Well, what *is* your type, then?"

Rick stopped laughing and looked suddenly serious in a way he rarely did. "Well," he said carefully, "first of all, my type is male."

I don't think there was anything in the world that would have shocked TJ more. His jaw dropped. His eyes popped and he just stared like Rick had slapped him across the face with a dead fish. I guess I could relate. When Rick had told me the year before, I'd been surprised. After all, Rick wasn't anything like those goofy stereotypes in the movies and sitcoms. At first, I admit, it totally weirded me out. I kept wondering if I was supposed to treat him differently, or if I was offending him somehow. But that got old pretty quick. He was still just Rick. My best friend who just happened to think that men were better-looking than chicks.

I knew, and Alexander knew, but poor TJ had been totally in the dark.

"Wha—" he tried. "Why?"

"Why am I gay?" asked Rick, grinning at TJ's discomfort. "Well, we don't really know. Some say it's genetic. Some say it's upbringing."

"No," said TJ, clearly struggling to keep his cool. "I mean, why didn't you tell me before?"

Rick got serious again. "Honestly? It's because before you started mooning over Jen5, I wasn't sure which team you were playing for."

"What?" TJ's eyes bugged. "You thought I was gay?"

He looked so funny saying it that I had to bite my tongue to keep from laughing.

"Yeah." Rick shrugged. "I've discovered that when another gay guy finds out that you're gay, they start taking liberties with you."

"You thought I would take *liberties*?" he said, and clearly he had no idea what Rick meant but was imagining something really horrible.

"I was just being cautious," said Rick. "Nothing personal. I'm not generally out, as they say."

"Wow," was all TJ could say.

Rick looked carefully at him, like he was trying to figure out what that "wow" meant. At last he said, "Are we cool?"

TJ nodded his head. "Yeah, for sure. I just . . . I've never known a gay guy before."

"Sure, you have." Rick grinned. "We've been friends since junior high."

"Hey, speaking of," I said. "Does Joe know you're gay?"

"Um," said Rick, "I think that's right up there with never introducing him to your mom."

"Gotcha," I said.

"But enough about me," said Rick, slugging down his beer. "Let's get back to the much more interesting topic: TJ's helpless crush on Jen5." He turned to Alexander, who was still cutting a swath of destruction through Halo. "Young Alexander, when did you first notice that our TJ was smitten?"

"Well, Richard," said Alexander, still not looking up

from his game, "I suppose it was a few days ago, during his fascinating but somewhat awkward description of the blindness of love."

"Ah." Rick nodded. "For me it was the vacant, frightened expression on his face whenever she sat down at our table." Then he turned to me. "And Samuel, what gave it away for you?"

"Can we just drop this?" I asked.

"Why?" asked Rick. He still had that weird grin like he was up to something devious.

"Sometimes when you get a little drunk," I said, "you get kind of mean like this and I don't think you realize it." Poor TJ looked like he wanted to curl up and die. He probably would have taken off for home right then and there, except it would have been hard to explain to his parents why he was coming home at midnight stinking of beer. "So don't be an asshole. TJ's had enough."

"TJ?" Rick asked, and the grin turned downright evil. "Who says I was picking on TJ?"

"What . . . ," I started. But then I finally got it. "Are you . . . ," I began. I just couldn't say it, though. I knew what he was suggesting, but it was just too . . . weird to think about.

"I'm just wondering," said Rick, "how it feels to have some competition."

"No," I said, and shook my head. "I do *not* have a crush on the Fiver."

Rick shrugged. "Maybe you do and maybe you don't. But she has *always* had a thing for you."

"No, fuck this," I said. "You're just trying to get me worked up."

"Alex," said Rick. "Back me up here."

Eyeballs still glued to the game, Alexander started chanting, "She wants to jump your bones!"

Rattattatt went the game.

"She wants to clean your pipes!"

Foosh went the game.

"She wants to ride your baloney pony!"

Ka-boom went the game.

"She—"

"Thanks, Alex," said Rick. "We get the idea."

I was so mad, I felt like breaking something. Maybe Rick's face. I couldn't think clearly and only said something dumb like, "You shitheads have totally lost it." But I felt more than just anger. There was another emotion. Like a chill or dizziness. Kind of like fear. "Fiver is like . . . She's my friend. My buddy . . ."

"Your *what* buddy?" said Rick.

I turned to TJ. Maybe just because I wasn't sure how

much longer I could hold off from punching Rick. "I'm sorry, TJ. You know Rick's just being a drunk shit."

But TJ was just kind of looking at me weirdly.

Rick continued. "You think Alex and I are making it up? So then you don't mind if TJ asks her out, right?"

I looked back and forth between Rick and TJ. In the background, Alexander was still blasting away bad guys. I wanted to say, *Yeah, sure, TJ, go ahead and ask Jen5 out,* all cool and nonchalant. *I hope you score.* But I couldn't say it. It stuck in my throat and wouldn't come out and I really felt like if I tried to force it, I would actually start crying or throw up or something.

So we stood there in silence, just staring at each other like gun fighters waiting for the other one to make the first move. Like that old Eastwood movie, *The Good, the Bad, and the Ugly.* I didn't know who was who, but I sure felt like we were in a desert.

Then the front door burst open.

It was Jen5.

"WHERE'S THE BEER!" she screamed.

We all stared at her. Even Alexander paused his game and turned around to look at her. She raised an eyebrow at us. "Wow, who died?"

"Hey, Fiver," said Rick calmly. "Beer's in the fridge."

"Thanks," she said, still watching us over her shoulder as she walked into the kitchen. "So . . . ," she said. "Did I miss something?"

"You sure did," said Rick. He seemed to have recovered from the shock already. He sprawled back onto the couch with his beer. "I was just telling TJ that I'm a big homo."

"Ah." Jen5 nodded. She gave TJ a sympathetic look. "Disappointing, isn't it? I always thought gay men were supposed to be smart and funny." She stood at the fridge and took a long chug on her beer. "And attractive," she added.

"You knew too?" asked TJ.

Jen5 rolled her eyes. "Please. I knew before he did."

The rest of the night was awful. We talked and joked and played more games like we always did. But every time I looked at Jen5, it was like I was seeing two people. One was my buddy. My confidante. Sure, Rick was my best friend, but he was so flaky that you couldn't really rely on him. Jen5 was the one I could always count on. But now there was this other person. A stranger. Not a pal, but a chick, and I suddenly had all the weird nerves and awkwardness that went along with hanging out with a chick. She even looked different. She was still the blond, gnarly-haired, crazy-dressing girl I'd always known. But now I couldn't help but check her out like she was a chick. She had boobs. When did she get boobs? And she wore tight jeans. When the hell had she started doing that? But it was other things too. Little things that really freaked me out. Like the way she looked at people with her eyes half closed and her head tilted, almost like a cat. And the way her lips curled up at the corners when she smiled, kind of mischievous and a little . . . sexy. I had never seen those things before. It made me feel like I had lost something important. Like I had lost a friend.

Toward the end of the night, she came and sat next to me and I couldn't help but tense up a little.

"How ya doing, Sammy?" she asked, patting me on the knee just like she'd done a million times before, but now it seemed suggestive.

"Okay," I said.

"You've been weirdly quiet," she said.

"Too drunk," I lied. What little buzz I had earlier was completely gone, and I'd been nursing the same warm beer since she'd shown up. The last thing I wanted was to feel overemotional or out of control. "I think I'm going to go to sleep," I told her, and got up. She said something else, but I wasn't listening. I slowly climbed the stairs and went into Rick's room. In the darkness I looked at the stupid car and sports posters on his walls. They were the same decorations he'd had since he was about twelve. I didn't think he even liked them anymore. He probably just hadn't bothered to take them down. But right then, I was glad because it was familiar. Comforting. It reminded me of when we were kids.

I lay down on the floor and stared up at the ceiling. My brain was buzzing again, even worse than usual. I kept thinking of Jen5's two identities and trying to merge them together. I thought of so many times in the past when Jen5 had reacted strangely to something, like making fun of my crush on Laurie, and now a lot of those moments made sense. But not in a comforting way. In a way that made me doubt I'd ever really known who she was at all.

I wasn't even asleep when Rick stumbled into the room hours later and flopped on his bed with a grunt. He passed out immediately. I listened to his snores for a long time after that. I couldn't help but wonder if Jen5 and TJ were still awake and what they were talking about. Or maybe they weren't talking. Maybe they were making out. Maybe they were . . .

The sun was just starting to come up when I finally fell asleep.

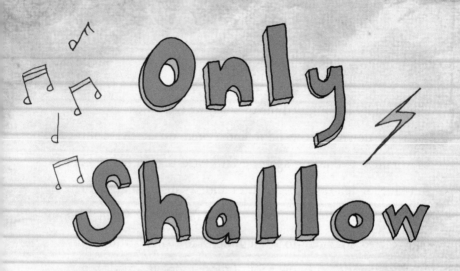

Only Shallow

5

Everyone else had alread split by the time Rick woke me up.

"Hey," he said, looking as rough as I felt.

"Hey," I said.

I took a shower, just to make sure I didn't have any beer residue on me before I went home. Afterward I came downstairs and saw Rick at the kitchen table, staring into a glass of orange juice.

"You mad at me?" he asked without looking up.

"No," I said.

"I'm sorry it came out the way it did," he said quietly. "In front of TJ and Alex like that."

"Okay," I said as I put my shoes on.

"But I'm not sorry I told you," he said. "I should have told you a long time ago."

I shrugged. I couldn't see how that would have made it any better. At least I'd been in blissful ignorance for a while.

"She really does like you," he said. "She told me. Of course, I wasn't supposed to tell you, but I just couldn't take it any longer. Hiding that from you."

"How did Alexander know?" I asked, although I wasn't sure why I cared.

"Alex seems kind of out there, but he notices a lot more than people realize."

"And TJ knew?"

"I'm sure. That was why he didn't do anything. We didn't talk about it or anything, but I think he felt like it would piss you off."

I nodded and walked toward the door.

"Do you like her?" he asked. "Like that?"

"I don't know," I said.

He nodded, like it was what he expected. Then, "See you tonight at rehearsal."

"Yeah," I said. "See you tonight."

"Morning, sweetheart," said my mom as I stepped into the house. She was reading the paper and sipping her coffee out of a massive travel mug like she always did. She drank a lot of coffee.

"Morning," I said, sitting down at the kitchen table.

"You had breakfast yet?" she asked.

"No," I said.

"Want something?"

"Sure," I said.

Mom almost never cooked dinner. I practically lived off of microwave meals. This was partially because she worked so late, but it was also because she was a terrible cook. Except for breakfast. On the weekends, it was like she tried to make up for all the family dinners we never had. She made pancakes, eggs, bacon, sausage, omelets, waffles, potatoes, oatmeal—you name it. Weekend mornings were a feast. And this morning was no exception. She must have been feeling a little extra energetic because she made my favorite: Scotch eggs. Hard-boiled eggs wrapped in bacon, then rolled in breadcrumbs and fried to a golden brown. Sound gross? Then you've never had them. They're the best.

"Thanks," I said as she served them.

"You okay, Sammy?" she asked.

"Sure," I said. "Why?"

"You just seem a little down."

"I am." There was no point in lying. She was a therapist, after all.

"Want to talk about it?"

"No," I said. Of course I did want to talk about it, but talking to my mother about girl problems was pretty much like torture. No matter what the conversation had originally been about, she would steer it toward sex and the need to protect myself, even if the girl said she was on the pill, because that wasn't any protection from HIV. And sometimes girls lied about the pill because they didn't want to break the mood and sometimes because they secretly wanted to get pregnant and trap guys into marriage. I guess because she thought I was some great catch? Who knows. She got a little weird about that stuff, so there was no way I was going to talk to her about this.

"Okay." She nodded. "Well, I'd like to talk about it if you change your mind." That was the therapist voice.

"Sure," I said. I even managed something that I hoped looked like a smile.

"You're only alone because you choose to be, Sam," she said quietly.

That sort of Dr. Phil statement always drove me nuts. My mom had a way of pushing my buttons. I guess, probably like all parents. But I felt like mine was a little better at it than most.

. . .

Clothes and smiles of rubber
Whore instead of lover
Talk with no conversation
Live with no realization

After breakfast, I wrote a verse of "Plastic Baby." I was beginning to wonder if maybe the song was about Laurie. Weird, huh? You'd think it would suddenly be about Jen5. But all this had got me thinking about what Jen5 had said about Laurie, and I wondered why I was into her. After all, looking objectively at it, she was a total trend-hound snob, and her dating Joe only confirmed that. Rich daddy's girl having a fling with the bad seed. But even though I knew all that, I still thought she was hot. Was I completely shallow? Did I want some hot chick who just agreed with everything I said? I didn't think so. And anyway, Jen5 was pretty hot too. Not as hot as Laurie, I guess, but still. And she was cool and someone I could talk to.

So why did trying to imagine myself dating her freak me out so much? I wanted to completely forget that I knew she wanted to be more than just friends. I wanted to not feel that confusion and weirdness and . . . fear. Nothing had changed, really. And yet everything had changed. And it could never be like it used to be.

Only Shallow

. . .

I wasn't sure what the deal with TJ was, whether he was jealous or angry or what. But I knew rehearsal was going to be weird. Sure enough, while we were getting set up later that afternoon, things were dead quiet. Then Joe came in, and with his incredible instinct for making things worse, he brought Laurie. She was dressed in some kind of super-hot black bodysuit that let you know exactly how perfect her body really was. To be face-to-face with Laurie while I was still struggling with the Jen5 stuff was almost more than I could handle. And why was she smirking? I felt kind of like she was laughing at us in her head.

Forget everything else, I thought. Just concentrate on the music.

But that turned out to be a problem as soon as we started up the first song. Rick didn't seem to remember what song we were playing. The rhythm matched up, but the actual notes were from a totally different song.

"Stop, stop, STOP!!!" yelled Joe.

The song ground to a halt.

"That sounded like crap!" said Joe. He punctuated his words by slamming his mic stand to the ground. "What the hell was wrong?"

We looked at Joe, then at each other.

"Rick," I said finally. "I think you were playing the wrong song."

"Oh," said Rick, but he didn't seem all that bothered by it. "I'm playing A-E-F-C."

"Right," I said. "But this song is F-C-F-C-G-D."

"Oh," he said again.

I thought I heard Laurie stifle a laugh, but when I turned, she looked more worried than anything else because Joe seemed like he was about to rip somebody's head off.

"What is wrong with you?" he snarled. "Permanent brain damage from too many whippits?"

This time, Laurie's giggle was unmistakable. She was actually laughing at Joe's stupid comment. And all at once, I saw that brainless preppy girl that Jen5 had told me about that no amount of dark lipstick and thick eye shadow could hide. Sure she was hot, but in the end she was just some dumb, snotty chick who always fawned over the big tough guy. Plastic baby, for sure. I was disgusted with myself for having wasted so much energy thinking about her.

But Rick wasn't fazed by either Joe's comment or Laurie's groupie act. He just said, "We going to start again or what?"

"Yeah, whatever," said Joe, and he stepped on the mic stand to bring it back upright.

TJ counted us in and we started over. Rick played the right

bass line. And you could always count on TJ. He was the best musician in the band, without a doubt. So after a little bit, the three of us finally found our groove together and it started to sound like a real song.

But then Joe began to sing. I glanced over and saw him holding the sheaf of lyric papers that I had typed up for him. He wasn't really reading from it too much though, just kind of mumbling something that sounded close to the words. He was too busy winking and thrusting his hips suggestively at Laurie, who giggled shyly with her hand over her mouth. Joe was paying so little attention to his singing that he actually started up on the third verse when we were supposed to go to the bridge. The three of us kept going, and it took him a few measures to catch on. When he did, his face immediately contorted from sly flirtation to absolute fury.

"WHAT ARE YOU DOING?!!!" he roared.

We stopped playing.

"What just happened there?" he demanded. This wasn't just Mean Joe. This was Mean Joe Impressing His Girlfriend.

Gramps once told me that fools rush in where wise men fear to tread. That was me all over.

"You went to the third verse," I said.

"Yeah?" he snarled, his eyes wide like some kind of psycho killer. "And?"

81

"It was time to go to the bridge," I said.

"Oh, well," he growled. "Excuse me!" He turned toward Laurie, waving the lyrics in the air above his head. "Maybe if these weren't the most asinine lyrics ever written, it'd be easier to remember them. I mean, come on." He held out the pages in front of him and began to read them like a lawyer or something. "'Make believe myself in a thirty-second drop, but I don't believe in fortune or my luck to stop'? Or how about, 'Fantasized fictional tragedy to feel. When all is said and done it seems like no big deal'? You asked what 'Tragedy of Wisdom' meant? Well, what the hell does *this* mean?"

I said, "It means—"

"SHUT UP!!! SHUT THE FUCK UP!" Joe's face was bright red now, and a thick vein stood out on his forehead. I don't think I'd ever seen him this angry. Or scary. "IT'S DUMB!" he yelled. "IT MAKES NO SENSE! All it does is rhyme because that's all you can do. But I guess we're stuck with you, now aren't we? So let's just start over again and see if we can somehow get this shit off the ground."

Total silence. It was one thing to crack on someone's clothes or hair or whatever. It was something completely different to knock the thing that someone sees as the most important thing in his life. My head was burning and I really wanted to just jump on him and pound him. I imagined my fists as sledgehammers beating him senseless. But part of me knew it wouldn't go like that. He was so much bigger and meaner than I was. He'd destroy me.

"Okay," I said quietly. "TJ, count us in again."

TJ clicked his drumsticks together and we started over. Rick fumbled for a second, but then got it together and the song started to pick up again. Joe glared at us, letting a full verse of music go by before he joined in. Then he went back to his mic and his pieces of paper and his winking at Laurie and the song limped on.

I didn't really feel like doing anything that night, but Rick didn't seem to care.

"Let's just go get some coffee at Idiot Child," he said as we walked through the Parks and Rec parking lot to the Boat.

"I won't be any fun," I told him.

"You never are," he said. "Anyway, I can't just let you go home, listen to Radiohead, and mope all night. Come on. Just you and me. It'll be a nice, quiet night."

I knew he was lying, of course. There was nothing nice or quiet about Idiot Child. It was a big, dark room full of broken-down couches and La-Z-Boy chairs. The air was so thick with cigarette smoke that you had to slouch in your seat and keep as low to the ground as possible, just so you could breathe.

And it was always packed with a smelly, grungy, angsty cross-section of Columbus's underground scene: skaters, punks, ravers, hippies, goths, and people who were just plain weird. But the coffee was cheap and surprisingly good, the music was always cool, and they let you hang out for as long as you wanted, as long as you bought something. For a dollar fifty, you had a place to hang for the whole night with no waitresses, cops, jocks, or parents to harass you. And it was worth all the rest just for that.

Plus, as a bonus, Rick and I knew the owner.

Francine was in her late twenties when her parents died in a car crash and left her with a ton of money. She spent it all on two things. One was a bunch of tattoos. She loved comics, and so she had her favorites—*Sandman, Emily Strange, Death Jr.,* and *Johnny the Homicidal Maniac* —inked on just about every inch of skin. And she was not a tiny person, so that was a lot of tattoos. One time she told me that she guessed she had about ten thousand dollars' worth of ink on her body. But she said it was worth it because she'd never liked looking at herself in the mirror before and now she did. She said it also scored with the chicks.

That was how we got to know Francine. When Rick realized that he was gay, he didn't tell his parents (they would totally freak). But he told our school guidance counselor,

Only Shallow

Mr. Liven, who was so cheery and unthreatening, you felt like you could tell him you'd just murdered a busload of nuns and he'd still be nice to you. Mr. Liven recommended that he join some kind of support group, I guess to talk with other gay people about being gay. Our neighborhood, German Village, was a pretty gay area, so he found a place that he could walk to after school. He went to a few meetings, and that was where he met Francine. Rick wasn't really into the meetings, because he said it was mainly a bunch of depressed old queens. Francine wasn't into it too much either. She'd hoped to meet some chicks, but she was the only lesbian there. So the two of them spent most of the time hanging out in the parking lot, smoking Francine's cigarettes and talking about comics. They both quit the group, and Francine said he should start hanging out at the coffee shop that she'd bought with the rest of her inheritance: Idiot Child.

Idiot Child was just as loud and smoky as usual. The only person who worked there besides Francine was Raef, a middle-aged dude with long red hair and a gnarly beard who filled in on Francine's nights off. He was standing behind the counter waving one hand in the air, the other pressed against the stereo receiver.

"Hey, kids," he said to us. "It's gonna take me a second to pour your coffee. I've almost got a clear broadcast."

We waited while he raised and lowered his body and waved his hand slowly back and forth. He had metal fillings in his mouth and a metal plate in his head and he claimed that if he positioned himself in just the right way, he could pick up radio signals in his brain and transmit them to the stereo. He said that the first time he'd discovered this ability, he'd accidentally channeled a Pink Floyd song, "Breathe," and it had changed his life forever.

But I guess it wasn't happening tonight. Eventually he gave up and said, "Just coffee, kids?"

We nodded. Neither of us had enough cash for a real espresso drink.

After we got our coffees, we sank into a couch in a corner of the room.

"I hope you didn't take what Joe said seriously," said Rick.

"What, about my songs being total shit?" I asked.

"Yeah," said Rick. "That. I think your songs are awesome."

"Even though you can't remember how to play them?" I asked.

"Yeah," said Rick. "That's why I'm bringing it up.

Because it's my fault that I can't remember them. I just haven't worked on them enough. And what I'm saying is that Joe hasn't either. He just doesn't want to admit it, so he's blaming you."

"I know," I said. "I mean, he'd probably say that stuff even if he loved my songs."

"Maybe he says it *more* when he likes them."

"I guess. Of course, I know they aren't brilliant, you know?"

"Sammy—"

"No, really. I'm still trying to figure out how to do it. I know that. I think it would help if we rehearsed more. And I feel kind of limited because I know there's some stuff I want to write that he would never sing because it's too emo or whatever."

"Sammy? Emo? No way!" Rick said.

"Do you think TJ is mad at me?"

"TJ will get over it," said Rick. "But you have to decide what you're going to do about Fiver."

"I really don't know what to do. For real."

"Do you think she's hot?"

"I've never thought about it before," I said. "She was just my friend, you know?"

"You gotta start thinking about it."

"Why? Why can't I just pretend you never said anything and go on being exactly like I was?"

"Well, first of all, there's TJ," said Rick. "He's only going to wait so long and then he's going to ask her out."

"Yeah," I said.

"And also, Fiver. She's only going to wait for so long before she gives up on you and finds someone new."

"She told you that?"

"Of course not. She's convinced she'll wait as long as it takes or she'll never date anyone. But I know better. And you know better. Fiver is not going to put up with this bullshit forever."

"I know.'"

"And it *is* bullshit, you know?" He leaned forward a little. "We've all be waiting for you two to hook up for years."

"Who's 'we'?"

"All of us. Shit, even your mom is waiting for it."

"You haven't talked to my mom about—"

"Of course not. I'm just saying that it's so obvious to everyone else that there's something there. Chemistry, magnetism, mojo. Whatever. It's present."

"I guess," I said, swirling the wooden stir stick in my coffee. "But it's just so . . . weird."

"What is?"

"Thinking about her like that. She's my friend."

"Are you seriously expecting me to believe that?" he asked, leaning back in his chair.

"What?"

"That you've never thought of her as anything other than a friend?"

"Yes."

"You would swear to me that you never once thought of her while jerking off."

"Jesus!"

"I'm serious. Can you tell me that?"

I said nothing.

"Exactly," said Rick, tapping the table like he had just scored a major point. "Now, look. Let me tell you what your real problem is."

"Oh, this'll be good," I said.

"Your problem is this: You freak out about the tiniest little stuff. You get all passionate and intense naming a stupid band or thinking about whether your favorite singer sold out or whatever. It's like life or death to you. But then when it comes to really important stuff, you totally puss out. It's like too much and you overload or something. It's time to grow some huevos, amigo. Be a man."

"What about you?" I asked.

"Huh?"

"When are you going to ask somebody out?"

"That's totally different," he said, shaking his head.

"No, I don't think it really is."

"There's no one for me to ask out," he said.

"Have you looked?" I asked.

"Just forget it," he said. "It's too weird talking about this."

"It's not weird at all. In fact, we were just talking about this stuff with me. You're just making it seem weird."

"Now, wait a minute," he said. "I brought you out tonight so that I could pick on you, not the other way around."

"Are you sure you're even gay?" I asked.

"What? Of course."

"Then why don't you ask someone out on a date?"

"Are you sure you're straight?" he asked.

"Of course."

"Then why don't you ask out the coolest chick in school when you already know for a fact that she'll say yes?"

"Oh," I said.

"Yeah," he said, folding his arms across his chest. "When I put it that way, it makes you feel a little stupid, doesn't it?"

How High the Moon

6

Sunday was a special day at my house. Sure, Mom only worked a few hours on Saturday, but that still meant nice clothes, hair, and makeup for her. So on Sunday, she sat around all day without makeup, in baggy sweats, and didn't leave the house. What this meant for me was that if anything needed to be done, like errands or shopping, I did it. I pointed out to her that the Starbucks coffee barista would probably forgive her if she showed up looking like a scrub once a week. But she just said it was a girl thing and I wouldn't understand.

Fortunately, we were pretty well stocked on the basics, so it was a quiet day until dinnertime. That's when one of Gramps's neighbors called and said he was acting weird. The neighbors were used to his normal weirdness, so anything they thought was unusual worried us. Someone needed to check it out. Usually, that someone was Mom. But since it was Sunday, that someone was me.

"I'm sure it's nothing," said Mom as she settled down on the couch for TV and ice cream.

When I pulled up in front of his building it was starting to get dark out, but I could still see what had worried the neighbors. Gramps had dragged a chair out onto the lawn in front of the apartment building. He was sitting with his hands in his lap, staring up at the sky between the building tops, looking totally at peace. And the strangest thing was that he was all dressed up correctly in a suit and tie. It looked like he'd even combed his hair.

When I opened the car door, I heard the last few bars of a song. The music ended and I saw him lean down and press the button on a small boom box at his feet. The music started up again and the smoky horn and lightly disjointed rhythm told me it was definitely Miles Davis.

He had returned his hands to his lap and he looked so still, I was afraid to startle him. But as I walked up the sidewalk, he turned calmly and looked up at me.

"Ah, Sammy," he said. "I knew you'd come. I knew she'd

send you. She's a smart one." He smiled quietly to himself. Then, "Have a seat."

Now that I was closer, I saw that he had actually brought out two chairs. Had he planned this?

"How long have you been out here, Gramps?" I asked as I sat down.

"As long as Davis's *Kind of Blue* album," he said. "I wonder why I can remember every note in that album but I can't remember who the president is." He sighed and looked back up into the night sky.

We sat there in silence for a little while. Then I said, "So why are you sitting here?"

"I'm looking for the moon," he said.

"The moon? It's right there." I pointed at the half-moon hanging in front of us.

"That?" he asked, his lip curling up a little. "That's a big rock with astronaut footprints that floats around in space."

There was another silence.

"Uh, yeah," I said. "That's the moon."

"When I was a boy, the moon was something different. It was magic. It was mysterious. Some people said a man lived up there."

"What?" I said.

"Haven't you ever heard of the man in the moon?"

"Well," I said. "That R.E.M. song . . ."

"What?"

"Never mind."

"Anyway, people believed there was a wise old man who lived on the moon. You could see his face on certain nights."

I looked up at the moon now. At the dark craters on its surface. Maybe sometimes the craters lined up in a way that looked kind of like a face. I couldn't see it, though.

"Other people," continued Gramps, "said aliens lived up there in giant subterranean caverns."

"Okay, now you're messing with me," I said.

He smiled and shook his head. "No one knew for sure because there was no way of knowing. Anything was possible." He rubbed his dry, wrinkled hands together and his face darkened. "But Kennedy needed a new measuring stick against the commies, some way to show America's dominance that didn't involve launching nukes, so they picked space. First one to the moon wins. And that night—that horrible night— when what's-his-name walked on the moon, that was the moment the moon's magic died. When it was no longer the moon. Just a rock floating in space." He scratched his beard slowly. Rhythmically. Then he said, "And I've been looking for the moon ever since." He turned to me then. "You're like me," he said. "Always reaching for the moon."

"Gramps, I know what the moon is."

He chuckled quietly. "Is that what you think? That you're just like everyone else? All the other boring farts out there just trying to live a sorry, carefree life? You might wish that were true. I can't blame you. Looking for the moon is hard. There's so many times when you've run out of hope and you feel like it's impossible. But it is possible. I know that for a fact."

He stared up into the sky for a little while, then said, "I know it because I touched it once. It was the night Chet Baker came to town and asked me to sit in on a set. Now, I know some people say he was a mediocre horn player and that he didn't really come into his own until he got his front teeth knocked out in a bar fight and had to do more singing and less playing. And maybe his playing wasn't the sharpest or most innovative. But that man knew where the music was. Where the moon was. And he showed me that night. Wouldn't let me fall back on my usual tricks of stylish trills and fancy footwork. He just kept shaking his head, right there in the middle of the set with an audience looking on and saying, 'Come on, Jack. You're more than that. Reach further. You can do it.' So I kept trying, kept ranging further out on solos and riffs and when it came around for me to take the Russ Freeman 'Summer Sketch' lead, I just pushed and pushed and I couldn't even believe what my fingers were doing and damn if he wasn't right. That song woke something up in me. It made me realize that there was something I'd been missing. And one thing I knew, I was going to hold on to it."

He shook his head. "But you can't. Not for long, anyway. Life beats it out of you real quick. So you just have to keep looking for it, over and over again. And you hope that someday you'll be able to hold on forever."

He closed his eyes and was quiet for a little while. So long, actually, that I started to wonder if he'd fallen asleep. But then he said, "It's a beautiful thing when you touch it. But there's an awful price to pay. Look what it did to me. And I'm one of the lucky ones." Then he opened his eyes and looked once more into the night sky and sighed. "But it was worth it. Such wonder. Such magic."

When I got home, Mom was sitting on the couch still, but the TV was off, and she had a glass of wine in one hand and a paperback novel in the other. I sat down next to her and waited for her to look up.

"How was he?" she asked.

"Really calm," I said. "I haven't seen him like that in a long time. I had almost forgot what he used to be like."

She nodded. "It comes and goes." Then she put down her book. She gave me her serious therapist look and put her hand on my shoulder. "He's slipping away from us, you know."

"Yeah," I said. "I guess I knew that. Do you think *he* knows?"

"Probably," she said. "Although when I've brought it up, he denies it." She took a sip of her white wine and stared out the dark window. "Imagine how awful that must be. To feel like you're slowly sinking into a confusing dream and to suddenly come up for air and everything is clear. But you know it won't last. That you'll sink back down, further and further each time, until you never come back."

I stared at the blank TV for a little while. Mom drank her wine.

"Do you ever worry?" I asked at last. "That you'll go crazy like him?"

She laughed. "Worry? I can't wait! Then someone else can listen to *me* ramble on for hours."

The thing that always bothered me about Sundays was that during the day it was a weekend, but at night it was a school night. It was hard enough to concentrate on homework other nights. But homework on a Sunday was almost impossible.

I had to write a short essay about *Macbeth*. Ms. Jansen gave us a question in our last class:

Do you think Macbeth was evil? Do you think he deserved his fate? Why or why not?

When I first thought about it, I was like, *totally.* He kills all these people just because he wants to be king. So I figured it was going to be a pretty easy essay to write. But then, as I sat down to actually write it, I started thinking something else. What gets him going down that path to killing everybody? Well, it's the witches telling him that he's going to be king. He wasn't even thinking about it before that. But once they plant that idea in his head, he gets excited about it. But even then, when it comes down to it, he still doesn't want to kill the king. But then his wife basically tells him that he's not a man unless he does it. So of course he does, because he's this dumb meathead jock who's a sucker for that kind of line. He's totally manipulated into the whole thing. And then things just keep getting worse and worse. He feels so bad about what he's done, but he isn't willing to fess up, so the guilt just drives him crazy. It's not that he's evil. He's just a wuss. He has this idea of what he *thinks* he wants, and he won't let that go, even though it's so incredibly obvious it's not turning out the way he wanted at all. So maybe he isn't evil, but anybody who refuses to do what they're supposed to do, just because it's not what they *thought* they wanted, deserves to get shafted.

Right?

Wait . . .

That's when I put down the pen and picked up the phone.

"Ah, the elusive Mr. Bojar!" said Jen5 when she answered.

"Hi," I said.

"I've called you three times this weekend. What's up, are you mad at me?"

I could tell by the way she said it that she was joking. But when I didn't say anything, she asked again, but quiet and a little worried-sounding.

"Are you?"

I'd been trying to think of how I was going to bring this up all day. All weekend, really. But I hadn't been able to think of anything, so I just asked point-blank, "Do you like me?"

"No, actually your mom pays me to be your friend," she said.

"No, I mean, do you *like* me?"

The silence was so long I wondered if she'd left the phone off the hook and just walked away. But finally she said, "We can't do this over the phone. Can you get out of the house right now?"

"Yeah," I said. "Sure."

"Meet me at the park in ten minutes."

Then she hung up.

I went downstairs. Mom was still in her chair reading, but at some point she had brought the whole bottle of wine out. I guess so she didn't have to walk to the fridge every time she needed to refill her glass.

"Mom," I said. "Can I go out for a bit?"

She looked at me in surprise, then looked at the clock, then back at me.

"Sammy, it's ten o'clock on a school night."

"Please, Mom," I said. "It's really important. It's . . ." I hesitated. I knew I had to make her understand that this was major and I wasn't just being a pain in the ass, but I really didn't want to talk to her about it. "It's . . . the thing that's been bugging me all weekend." Was that enough?

She regarded me carefully, I guess trying to read if this was teenage BS or the real deal. At last she said, "Okay, Sammy. But be smart."

"Thanks, Mom," I said. Then for some reason, it just came out of my mouth: "Thanks for trusting me."

She looked like I'd just said something insanely shocking. Then, even weirder, it looked like she was suddenly about to cry. She blinked rapidly and smiled.

"Get out of here, kid," she said hoarsely.

How High the Moon

• • •

Jen5 and I used to hang out at Schiller Park a lot before I got the Boat, since it was within walking distance for both of us. It was pretty big. A huge playground, a rec center, basketball courts, a pond stocked with fish, even an outdoor amphitheater where they did Shakespeare every summer. She and I had spent a lot of summer afternoons in that park, just hanging out and talking about parents, friends, movies, music, art, books, whatever. We'd stay until after sunset. Sometimes a cop showed up after dark and kicked us out. He always looked kind of disappointed that we weren't doing anything bad. But those were simpler times, when we were more excited about the new Johnny Depp movie than about sex and beer.

When I got there, I could see Jen5's silhouette against the bright white security lights. She sat on a swing, swaying back and forth and dragging her feet a little in the gravel. I walked over and sat in the swing next to hers. We were quiet for a while. The creak of the swing chains was loud in my ears.

Then Jen5 said, "So I guess Rick wasn't talking about being a homo when I showed up on Friday."

"He was talking about that, too," I said. "But that wasn't what we were talking about when you came in."

She nodded and let the swing shift back and forth some

more. Then she said, "I wasn't trying to keep anything from you. I was just worried that if I brought it up, it would make things weird between us."

"Like it is now," I said.

"Yeah," she said. Her bright paisley eyes gleamed in the harsh lighting. "Look, if we were . . . together . . . God, that sounds so lame. Whatever. Anyway, if we *were*, the way I see it, things wouldn't be that much different, really."

"What?"

"Think about it. We'd still be friends. But instead of talking all the time, we just talk *most* of the time and then, you know . . . make out and stuff the rest of the time."

For a moment I couldn't quite understand what she was saying. It was like my brain had to back out from the spot where it was parked, turn around, and pull into this new spot that I hadn't seen before. The way she explained it seemed so reasonable.

"I mean," she went on. "We're both virgins, right? And I don't know about you, but I'd sure to like to . . . try some stuff. You know?"

"Uh," I said. "Yeah." My heart was suddenly pounding so hard, I could literally feel it in my throat.

"So, wouldn't it be better to try stuff with someone you trust? With someone you . . ."

She looked away, stared hard at her shoes.

It took a second for me to get enough saliva back in my mouth to talk. And when I did, all that came out was, "What?"

"I mean," she said quietly, "Unless you just don't see me that way."

Maybe this is terrible and means that secretly I'm a total dick. Or maybe it's just one of those things that's human nature. Either way, her sudden weakness made me feel stronger. It made me feel, for the first time, like I was the one in control of this situation. And that feeling gave me the confidence to make a choice.

I lunged across the swing chain and kissed her.

At first it totally didn't work. I pretty much just mashed my face against hers. Stupid and clumsy and not sexy at all. We both got tangled in the swing chains and then we just kind of fell over onto the ground in a heap. But that didn't stop us. We just kept on going. And kissing Jen5 felt a lot different from how I thought it would. Usually her attitude was always kind of hard and rough, so I guess I expected her kiss to feel rough too. But instead, she felt soft and warm in a way that I didn't even realize she could be. It made me think that there were so many things I didn't know about her. So many things I didn't understand. And yet she was my best friend. While we kissed in the gravel under the fluorescent lights in the park, the two Jen5s—my buddy and the hot chick—merged into one really amazing girl.

Then a bright light hit my face. I pulled away quickly.

"Wha—" Jen5 said. Then she saw.

A cop stood at the entrance, shining his flashlight at us.

"Park's closed," he said. "You kids go on home."

He looked very pleased with himself.

I Just Wanna Get Along

7

The next day at school, Jen5 insisted

on holding hands in the hallway and other goofy dating stuff.
At first, I told her no way. But she said it was an experiment. I
didn't understand what she meant exactly, but I played along.
So there we were, walking around holding hands all day like a
couple of complete tools. I thought for sure we'd get all kinds
of comments. But we didn't. No one seemed to notice, even.
I guess because we always hung out together anyway, most of
the school just assumed we'd already been dating.

On the drive over to rehearsal, I told Rick that Jen5 and I
were officially dating.

All he said was, "About time."

"Why am I the only person that didn't see this coming?"
I asked.

"Do you know what an idiot savant is?" asked Rick.

"I'm pretty sure you're going to tell me, and it's going to be insulting," I said.

"Kind of. It's someone who's really good at one thing and sucks at everything else."

"Oh, right, like I'm such a brilliant musician that I'm totally clueless about everything else."

"Nah, I was thinking that you're really brilliant about being an idiot about girls."

"That's why I have a gayfriend," I told him. "You can advise me because you're more connected to your feminine side."

Rick raised an eyebrow. "*Gayfriend*?" he asked.

"I just made it up," I said.

"I can tell. And anyway, sullen emo boy, you're way more feminine than I am. I'll bet you even shower daily."

"Uh . . . yeah," I said. "You don't?"

He leaned back in his seat, looked out the window, and smirked. "My natural scent is far more appealing."

"To who?" I asked.

The Parks and Rec building where we rehearsed was downtown in an old, faded blue cement-block structure with hardly any windows. There were lots of meeting rooms, a gym, and probably a lot of other stuff I didn't know about. The only thing that I really cared about was the old dance studio in the back where we rehearsed.

As soon as we walked through the heavy front door of the building, we could hear the sound of hard drumming coming from all the way down the hall.

I looked at Rick.

He shrugged and said, "Guess TJ found out about you and Fiver."

"That's way too loud," I said. "We're totally going to get yelled at." We were always getting yelled at by people who worked there. It seemed like they might be getting pretty close to kicking us out.

"Come on," I said. "We better quiet him down before Joe gets here."

We stopped in front of the closed door to the dance studio and just stood there for a second, listening to TJ totally murder the drum kit.

"You have to admit," said Rick. "Romantic angst seems to work for him. He sounds like he's on fire in there."

"This is going to be awkward, isn't it?" I asked.

There was a crash from inside that was so loud, it sounded like TJ had split a cymbal in half.

"What gives you that idea?" asked Rick.

I opened the door and hot, sweaty air slapped me in the face, followed by the unmuffled sound of TJ whaling on his kit in a way I didn't even think he was capable of. The bass felt like a kick in the chest, the cymbals like needles in my ears, the snare like a punch in the mouth, and the whole thing came together like someone had just stuck my wet finger in an electrical socket. I almost couldn't believe it was really him. His T-shirt was off and wrapped around his head in a makeshift headband to keep sweat out of his eyes. He was usually way too skinny, hunched, and zitty to get away with being shirtless, but at that moment it was just part of a picture of a guy totally plugged into his music and kicking the shit out of his inner demons. I knew I was supposed to stop him. Calm him down. But this was what Gramps had been talking about. In that moment, I was witnessing TJ touch the moon. And how could you stop something that clearly brilliant and still call yourself a musician? So Rick and I just drifted into the room, mesmerized by the sound and raw power.

"STOP!"

TJ jerked to a halt, his eyes a little glazed.

Joe stood in the doorway, his face a reddish-purple snarl. Laurie stood a little bit behind him, cringing like a puppy.

"Are you all idiots?" screamed Joe. He stalked into the room, his chains making little *ching* sounds with each step of his steel-toed boots. His fists were clenched so tight that the knuckles were white. "Do you *want* us to get kicked out of here?"

"Sorry," said TJ as he mopped sweat off his face. He didn't seem bothered by Joe's tantrum. In fact, he seemed even more relaxed and peaceful than usual.

Joe stalked closer. "If we get kicked out of here because of your dumb ass," he said, getting right up in TJ's face, "I will take you apart."

"Okay," said TJ, utterly indifferent.

Joe stood there, glaring at him for a moment, his jaw grinding back and forth, his forehead pushed forward in a caveman frown. TJ just adjusted his cymbals and snare, which had gotten a little out of whack during his extended drum solo. He didn't even seem to notice that Joe was right in front of him, ready to throw him through the mirrored wall.

After a few incredibly long moments of silence, Joe said, "Put your shirt back on, you scrawny faggot." Then he spun around on his heel and walked over to his mic stand. Laurie sat down on a stool next to him, but her eyes were on TJ. She was staring at him with a wide-eyed expression, like she had never seen him before. Maybe Joe noticed too, because he tapped her on the forehead with his finger and said, "Hey."

She flinched a little, then looked up at him.

"Get my songbook," he said, and gestured over to the door where he had dropped his bag.

As she walked over and started rummaging through it, he turned back to us.

"Okay," he said. "After Saturday's suckfest, I decided it was time for me to take charge of things. Maybe that's been the whole problem. You guys clearly need a leader. I thought maybe you could handle at least *some* of the responsibility, but I guess not."

At this point, Laurie came back with a little notebook. He took it from her and started flipping through it. She went and sat back down on her stool.

"Uh," I said. "Joe, what are you talking about?"

"I'm talking," said Joe, still flipping through his notebook, "about dragging you guys kicking and screaming into being a real band. Starting with"—he stopped and looked at a specific page in his notebook, then turned the page in my direction. Like I could read his handwriting from five feet away—"new songs."

A strangled noise came from Rick. I looked over at him and he was frowning and chewing on his lip. That was what he always did when he was trying not to laugh. I turned back to Joe.

"New songs?" I asked. I had to have misheard him.

"Yeah," he said. "You're not the only one who can write music, you know."

"Right," I said.

"What's the matter, Sammy? Can't handle a little challenge? Afraid someone else could be a better Conor Oberst wannabe?"

"Uh, no, Joe," I said. "If you wrote a song, that's cool." I didn't say that because I was scared of him. It was because I just couldn't believe that he had actually written something. "Let's hear it."

Joe smirked like he had just won some major victory. "Let me see your guitar." Then he held out his big, meaty hand.

"My guitar?"

"I'm not going to sing a cappella, you idiot," he said. "Come on, Gollum. I won't hurt your Precious."

I must have been in shock by that point, because I actually handed over my '61 Gibson SG reissue. Joe grabbed it by the neck with a rough carelessness that made me wince. Gramps always said that a man treats his instrument like he treats his woman. Looking at Laurie, huddled meekly in the corner, it looked like Gramps might be right on that one.

Joe slung the strap over his head and plugged in. Then he let out a few dirty chords. Not that I'm some chord purist, but if you're playing them open and letting them ring out, they should probably sound like a bunch of notes that go together. But he nodded to himself, pleased.

"My stuff is real hardcore," he said. "You guys are going to shit your pants when you hear this."

"Probably," muttered Rick quietly.

"You want a pick?" I asked, fishing around in my pocket for one.

"Nah, that's why I have such a long thumbnail. I don't need a pick." He held up his thumb to show us. I hadn't noticed before, but it was really long. And dirty yellow.

"Wow," said Rick. "Just . . . wow."

"Shut up and listen," said Joe. Then he let out another half-tuned chord and began to sing in a slow, heavy, measured beat, *"Welcome to the sanity closet, you know we are here!"*

There was a pause as he changed his fingering on the guitar to a different chord. Then he strummed again. *"Pulling down the wishful thinking of the young in years!"*

Another slow chord change.

"Stepping down on their emotions, heedless of their tears!"

Another chord change, but it went sour. Joe cursed under his breath, adjusted his fingers, then tried again, this time mostly right.

"Greeting their pleas of mercy with a thousand leers!"

Then he just banged at the open strings, screaming "REFORM!" over and over again for a few minutes.

"And you get the idea," he said, waving his hand at us. "That's just the first verse. Obviously, I'm not a guitar player really. It was just to give you an idea. So?" He looked at us, half expectant, half daring us to say something negative.

"Uh . . . ," said TJ.

"Who knew," said Rick. "Who knew you were capable of . . . that."

Joe's face crinkled up into a snarl. "You know what, fuck you guys. I'm out of here." He practically threw my guitar at me and I barely managed to keep from dropping it.

"Come on, Laurie," he snapped.

Then he grabbed his bag and started walking to the door.

"Wait," I said.

He stopped.

"Come on, man, don't be like that," I said. "We can work with this."

I heard a hoarse "What?" escape from Rick's throat. I ignored him and looked pleadingly at TJ to back me up, hoping he understood that if Joe walked out that door, Tragedy of Wisdom was dead. Then I turned back to Joe.

"It's not really our sound, okay, sure," I said. "But maybe we can work it in. Maybe we can meet in the middle somewhere."

"Yeah." TJ nodded, a little unsure. "A totally new sound no one's ever heard before."

"Or would want to hear again," muttered Rick.

"Seriously, Joe," I said. "Let's at least try."

He let us squirm for a full minute before he finally rolled his eyes, dropped his bag on the floor, and came back over.

"Yeah, okay," he said, like it didn't really matter. "It was just a basic structure, of course. I expect you guys to fill in the details and stuff."

"Exactly," I said. "So what were those chords? E-A-G-A?"

"Okay," Rick said during the drive back home after rehearsal. "What I want to know is, how do you greet somebody with a thousand leers?" Then he burst into the belly laugh he had been holding in for hours.

"I know, I know," I said. "It's just one song."

"I don't believe you," he said. "You were throwing a fit about him naming the band, and now you're letting him write a song? What is wrong with you?"

"I just . . . ," I started. "He was going to walk out of the band. That would have been it. No more band. I *need* a band."

"But we don't need him," said Rick. "He sucks. You should be leading anyway."

I Just Wanna Get Along

"We've talked about this a million times," I said. "I can't sing in front of people."

"That was just the one time. At that crappy open mic."

"It was the *only* time," I said.

"Oh, come on," he said. "It wasn't that bad."

"It was the most embarrassing moment of my life."

"Sammy, you just have to—"

"No," I said. "I don't want to talk about it."

Monkey Gone to Heaven

8

I needed to talk to TJ and I knew it
would be weird and awkward and I didn't want to do it. But
I also didn't want that weirdness in the band anymore. And if
I could suck it up and let Joe contribute a song for the good
of the band, I could at least talk to TJ about me dating Jen5.

The next day, TJ and I were lab partners in biology. The two
of us stood in front of a table and stared at the formaldehyde-
stinking clam in a dish. We were supposed to dissect it and
label each part, but it was hard to know where to begin, since
it just looked like a big slimy lump.

TJ prodded it with the scalpel experimentally. "I think this
might be its stomach," he said without much confidence.

"Look, TJ," I said. "About me and Fiver . . ."

TJ nodded, looking about as uncomfortable as I felt. But I forced myself to go on.

"You know this wasn't planned," I said. "And I didn't mean to . . ." What? I wasn't exactly sure what I had done wrong, but I really wanted TJ to be cool with it.

"No, it's great," said TJ. "Really. I mean, you and Five are, like, perfect for each other. And you've been friends forever . . ."

"Yeah," I said. I felt like he wanted to say more, so I waited.

"I mean," he said, "I *was* upset. Especially since it took someone else being interested to make you step up. But then, after rehearsal yesterday . . ." His eyes darted everywhere in the room except to me. He chewed on his lower lip.

"Yesterday?" I prompted.

"Laurie called me up and asked if I wanted to hang out."

"What?"

"And we did. And it was really cool. *Really* cool."

"Laurie?" I repeated. "You. And Laurie?"

TJ shrugged. "You and I have the same taste in girls."

"Wow," was all I could say.

"So I guess . . . ," TJ began, before throwing up his hands. "I don't know. I hope you're cool with that."

"Yeah," I said, not really sure until the words came out of my mouth. "Yeah, actually I'm totally cool with that."

"Really?" asked TJ.

"Really," I said. "Weird as that is." Then I realized what that meant for the band. "So, does Joe know?"

"I don't think so," he said. "But things get around . . ."

"Right," I said. "He's going to shit himself."

"Yeah," said TJ. He looked at me pleadingly. "But what am I going to do? Tell her we can't date?"

"You're not really asking me that," I told him.

"No," he agreed. "I'm not."

She *was* the hottest chick in school, after all.

"We'll figure something out," I told him.

We turned our attention back to the clam, comparing our diagram to the blob.

"Maybe that's a lung," I said.

"Oh, I thought it was the foot," said TJ.

"Hmm," I said. "You might be right."

We poked at it a little more.

"Oh," said TJ. "Both Joe and Rick stopped me in the hallway and said they couldn't make it to rehearsal tonight."

"What?! Do they know the contest is only a week away?"

TJ shrugged.

"Why don't they tell *me* these things?"

"Probably because you'd react like this," said TJ.

"I can see that with Rick, but I seriously don't think Joe cares how I react to anything."

"I wouldn't say that," said TJ. "But then, I don't think you notice what kind of effect you have on other people anyway."

"What's that mean?"

"I don't know. I guess that you don't give yourself enough credit. After all, you're the only thing that's keeping this band together."

"That's supposed to make me feel better?" I asked.

TJ shrugged and poked at the clam some more.

"This sucks," I said. "I was really in the mood to play tonight."

"Me too," said TJ. "You wanna come with me to play over at Alexander's house?"

"With Alex?"

"Of course."

"What's he going to play? His hand farts?"

"No," said TJ, surprised. "Didn't you know? He plays bass."

"Alexander plays bass?" I repeated.

"He's pretty awesome, too."

"You've played with him before?"

"A couple of times."

"Why didn't I know he played bass? Why didn't he ever mention it?"

"You know. It's Alex. He's a weird dude. So how about it?"

"Sure," I said. "Let's just jam."

"Cool." TJ nodded. Then he hesitated. "Laurie's going to come along. Maybe you wanna invite Jen5?"

"I can ask her," I said. "But she usually isn't interested in tagging along to a rehearsal."

But when I asked her after school, she *was* interested.

"Really?" I said.

"Yeah." She nodded. "Sounds like fun."

"You've never wanted to come to practice before."

She let out a huge sigh, like she couldn't believe I was so dense. "That's because Joe was there. You know I can't stand that guy."

"Oh," I said. Then, "Well, Laurie's going to be there."

"That's fine," she said.

"I thought you didn't like her."

"I didn't like you liking her," she said. "Now that I don't have to worry about it, she's cool." Then she raised an eyebrow and said, "But what are you going to do about Joe?"

"I don't know," I admitted. "Maybe he broke up with her and doesn't really care who she dates."

"Yeah, that sounds real likely," she said.

"Maybe he's so blinded by the joy of getting to contribute songs, he won't even care."

"You're letting him write songs for the band now?" she asked.

"I don't want to talk about it," I said.

I'd never been to Alexander's house before. He lived a little farther from school in one of the suburbs with big houses and big yards and no sidewalks. I tried to avoid going to places like that as much as possible. When Jen5 and I got there, TJ's car was already parked out front. We knocked on the door and Alexander answered.

"Hey, guys. This is great! Nobody but TJ ever comes this far out."

We got a brief glimpse of the rest of the house. It had that warm, homey feel, with lots of knickknacks scattered everywhere. But we didn't spend much time in the rest of the house, because Alexander led us down to his furnished basement.

It was like walking down a set of narrow wooden steps and finding paradise. There was a big TV, a game console, a huge stereo, a brand-new Apple computer, and just about every kind of musical instrument and piece of music equipment you could think of.

TJ was already warming up, just playing a light little combo. Laurie was sitting on a couch watching him. She had gone through some kind of makeover since the night before. She'd switched out the goth princess look for some kind of glam retro '80s thing that went perfectly with TJ's modboy hipster look. That wasn't the only change, though. She also looked kind of . . . happy. Jen5 plopped down next to her and they started chatting like they were buddies.

Alexander showed me where to plug in. He handed me a cord and my eyes followed the sleek, clean rubber casing to the amplifier that had more knobs and switches than I knew what to do with. Then my eyes followed the cables from the amp to a full, beautiful speaker stack that was to be the conduit for my sound.

Then he said, "Here's a pedal board." He handed me a shiny piece of rectangular chrome and black plastic. It had four pedals on it and more little knobs and switches. "It's kind of simple," he said. "But it's got all the basics: distortion, flange, chorus, and echo. And it's really easy to use."

What did I say? Paradise.

While I was setting up, Alexander strapped on his bass and started playing. TJ had been right. Alexander really was good. He and TJ didn't have much in common as people, but listening to them play a simple rhythm section, you could feel that rare kind of rapport between a drummer and bassist that gave every song a solid groove. When I joined in, skimming a melody off the top of their jam, it was so easy because they gave me so much. I understood in that moment something that Gramps had told me over and over again. That you had to be able to trust everyone playing in your band.

When we were taking a little break, I said, "We're playing kind of loud. Are your parents home?"

"They are," said Alexander.

"Do you think they mind?" I asked.

Alexander shrugged. "The basement's soundproof."

Heaven.

"So who's going to sing?" asked Alexander. "I have a mic with a stand."

We looked at one another. We looked at the girls on the couch.

"No way," said Laurie.

"I don't know any of your music," said Jen5.

"Why don't you sing, Sammy?" asked TJ. "You know all the words to everything. Don't try to tell me you don't."

"But I can't sing very well," I said.

"You sound better than Joe."

"Yeah, but I don't—"

"Oh, shit, you're just fooling around anyway!" said Jen5. "No record label guys are hiding behind the stereo."

"Yeah, Sammy," said Alexander. "Come on. Someone's got to do it."

"Okay, okay," I said. I was totally blushing and at first it was hard to relax, sing, and still play guitar. But after the first few songs and nobody laughed, I actually started to have fun with it.

And what did we play? Pretty much everything, from the more pop kind of stuff like Arcade Fire and Death Cab for Cutie, to established stuff like Tom Waits, Modest Mouse, Dinosaur Jr., Soul Coughing, and the Jesus and Mary Chain. Alex knew them all. I even pulled out more obscure bands like Neutral Milk Hotel, Mercury Rev, My Bloody Valentine, and Sparklehorse. Most of those he knew too. And the best thing was, if he didn't know them, after listening to a little bit of it, he would just make up something that was pretty close. It was unreal. A musical genius right under my nose, and I never knew it.

I thought it would be weird having Jen5 and Laurie there, but they made it even better. Laurie was really smiling now, laughing and cheering us on. And Jen5? Well, as much as I wanted to be a rock star, I'd never really felt like one. But that night, when I saw how she looked at me, I felt like a musical genius myself. I felt like I could do just about anything. And while my experience in dating was kind of slim, I was pretty sure that having someone who made you feel like that was worth a lot.

The only bad part of the night was afterward, when we'd said good night and thanked Alexander's parents for having us over and saying that we'd have to do this again really soon (and meaning it). Jen5 and I walked to the Boat and left behind the warm, cozy feeling of that basement paradise.

"What's up?" she said.

"Nothing."

"Lies."

"I don't know," I said. "It's just . . . this was really nice."

"Yeah," she said. "It was."

"I don't think something like that could ever happen with Tragedy of Wisdom. Not even if we practiced every night for hours."

"No," she said. "Probably not."

"I wish this was the band I was in."

"Why can't it be?"

"What about Rick?"

"I think he'd get over it."

"What about Joe?"

"Screw Joe," said Jen5.

"We'd need a singer."

"You did great tonight. You were awesome."

"I can't be a frontman."

"Jesus, Sammy, how many times do I have to tell you, yes you can."

I shook my head. "I can't."

She stopped and grabbed my arm. "Seriously. Why is this such a hang-up for you?"

"You wouldn't understand," I said.

"Oh, it's too deep for me or something?"

"No," I said. "That's not it at all."

"I'm not Mr. Tortured Artist, so I wouldn't get it?"

"No, it's . . ."

"What? Just tell me!"

"It scares the shit out of me, all right? I can play guitar in front of people because I just concentrate on my guitar and pretend there's no one there. But singing, you have to *look* at the audience."

"But if you just tried—"

"I did try. Rick talked me into this open mic a while back. I walked on that stage, started to play, but I was so nervous, my throat just closed up. I couldn't sing a single note. I vamped for a minute like a complete jackass with everyone staring up at me, wondering what the hell I was doing. Then I just gave up and walked offstage. And the worst part? The quiet pity applause." I looked at her. "There. Now you know. Happy?"

She just stared at me with this confused look on her face, her paisley eyes wide, her mouth open a little.

"See, I knew you wouldn't understand," I said. "You just go into everything fearlessly, like a friggin' Mack truck. Well, not everybody can be like you, okay?"

We drove home in total silence. I think it was the first time I ever got the last word on Jen5 like that. A few weeks ago, that would have given me some kind of weird satisfaction. But something was different now. I didn't like the defeated silence. After a little while, I wanted to break it.

But I just didn't know how.

Caring Is Creepy

9

The next day at school, things were still really tense between me and Jen5. For most of the day, we did our best to avoid each other. But at lunch, I refused to leave the table and I guess so did she. The two of us ate in silence, purposely not looking at each other, as Rick and Alexander grilled TJ mercilessly on what it was like to date Laurie.

"So, does she have, like, weird body hair somewhere?" asked Alexander.

"I bet she's like a Barbie, without nipples or anything," said Rick.

"No, there was this one day she was wearing a white T-shirt and it started to rain and I definitely saw nipples," said Alexander.

Caring Is Creepy

"Do you, like, worship at the Temple of Laurie every night?" asked Rick.

"Does she require animal sacrifices?" asked Alexander.

"I bet she likes to talk dirty," said Rick.

"I bet she recites presidential speeches!" said Alexander.

"What?" Rick turned to him.

"I don't know . . . ," Alexander said, and shrugged.

TJ just took it the way he usually did, with complete calm. He did have a slight smirk, though. He knew this was like their way of congratulating him. Of course, usually at some point during these riffs, Jen5 would rein Rick and Alex in before they got too offensive. But today she just sat there and ate her sandwich, her arms pulled in to her sides and her head a little bowed, like she was cold. Like she didn't want to be bothered.

I felt guilty, but I couldn't figure out why. It wasn't like I had said anything insulting. If anything, it had been a compliment. She usually *was* fearless. But it felt like I had really let her down somehow. And now I didn't know what to do.

"I mean," I said to Rick on the drive to rehearsal that afternoon, "am I supposed to apologize for being a pussy or something? Or, now that she knows I'll never be some hunky lead-singer type, she's rethinking wanting to date me?"

"I can't figure out why she's so upset," said Rick. "I've *always* known you were a pussy."

"Jesus, can't you be serious just this once?"

"Seriously, I don't know, dude."

"About Jen5?"

"About whether I can be serious."

"See, this is when a *real* gayfriend would come in and explain things from her point of view."

"Sorry I'm not conforming to your stereotype," said Rick, putting his feet up on the dashboard. "It must be awfully disappointing."

"Dude, get your jankey sneakers off my dash."

"What is up your butt today?" said Rick.

"Nothing," I said. "I think I'm going to get dumped by my girlfriend after only dating a few days, and I'm driving to another shitty band rehearsal for a competition where we plan to make total asses of ourselves in front of the entire local music scene. It's nothing at all."

"Wow," said Rick. "Tonight's going to be interesting."

We were really sucking at rehearsal. Rick was playing the wrong song once again and Joe still didn't know the lyrics or much of the melody to any of the songs I'd written. We flubbed around for a little, trying to keep the song going, but a little more than halfway through, it just kind of fell apart. There was a long silence. Then Joe said, "What the fuck were you doing, TJ?"

TJ looked surprised. "What do you mean?"

"Shit." Joe threw his hands up in frustration, like any idiot could see it. "How can the rest of us play if you can't keep the stupid beat?"

TJ frowned and seemed to actually be wondering if his tempo had been off. But I realized what was going on here. And I was in exactly the right mood to butt in.

"Leave him alone, Joe. You know he's playing better than any of us."

"What do *you* know about it?" said Joe.

"Well, I wrote the song," I said. "So I guess I kind of know what it's supposed to sound like."

"Oh, right." Joe rolled his eyes. "These brilliant songs you wrote. Such quality stuff. It's like we have our own little Thom Yorke here."

Normally this was where I could just roll my eyes at his stupid joke like I had so many times before, and that would be the end of it. But not this time.

I said, "We all know why you're *really* on TJ."

Joe's face went hard immediately and he took a few steps toward me, his fists clenching and unclenching. "What do you know?" His voice was just a harsh growl.

"Uh, Sammy . . . ," I heard Rick say. He sounded worried. Almost afraid. But I didn't care. This band sucked and nobody in it was trying, so fuck it. One word would blow it up.

"Laurie," I said.

It happened so fast that I didn't even think about it. I saw Joe's face curl up and his shoulder slant, saw his arm draw back while his fist clenched. Then he came at me with a big roundhouse punch. I dodged to the side. His knuckles cracked into the cement wall behind me. It sounded like someone stepping on a dry tree branch. Broken bones.

He fell to the floor holding his fist and screaming, "Oh, shit! Oh, shit!" But what I was still hearing was that breaking sound. I watched him writhe on the ground. There was blood. And maybe that was bone sticking out of his knuckle.

But I didn't feel anything.

"Jesus, Sammy," said TJ. "What should we do?"

"I guess I'll take him to the hospital," I said. My voice sounded strange in my ears. "Rehearsal's over."

I drove Joe to the emergency room. The whole way there he swore at me and insulted me and Jen5, although you could tell he didn't know her well enough to come up with anything really offensive. But he knew me pretty well.

"You think you're so deep?" he snarled. "You're a total

poser. A nothing. Your songs are crap and you're such a little shit, you'll never get anywhere or do anything."

But what he said didn't bother me. I felt completely in control. And by the time we got to the hospital, he had settled down into a sulky silence. I parked the Boat in one of the hourly spots in the garage. He had been staring at his purple-and-red, swollen, bloody hand, but when we came to a stop, he looked around, confused.

"This isn't the drop-off," he said with the authority of someone who had been dropped off at the ER many times.

"Right," I said. "I'm going in with you."

"Forget it," he said quietly. "I know what to do from here."

"I'm going in with you," I said again, still calm, still cool.

He looked at me for a second, like he was going to tell me to piss off or something. He might have been in too much pain to argue, or maybe it was something else, but finally he just shrugged and said, "Whatever." Then, cradling his broken hand to his chest, he got out of the Boat and started walking to the ER entrance. He didn't look back to see if I was following.

It took me a minute to adjust, walking from the gathering darkness outside into the bright fluorescent world inside. I blinked and looked around at the brown-and-yellow room. It was quiet and grim and felt a little seedy. A TV showed an infomercial for prayer cloths that would get you anything you wanted. People sat slumped and sad, like they had always been there, waiting to be fixed by the doctors. Like they always would be there. I watched Joe walk up to the counter and saw that he was sad and slumped also. Like he was one of them. I took a seat while Joe talked with the woman at the desk. After he'd struggled to fill out the paperwork with his good hand, he walked back and sat down next to me.

"They never take you right away, unless your life is in danger," he said.

I nodded but didn't say anything. I thought maybe I was supposed to apologize or something. But I wasn't sorry. I wasn't anything. So I just sat there.

After a while, Joe said, "I really liked her."

I nodded.

"I guess too much, maybe," he said.

He wasn't looking at me. Just staring off into the distance, still as sad and slumped as the rest of them. "You know, it was a weird feeling and I didn't know what to do with it. So I got angry."

I wondered if he was talking about trying to punch me, or picking on TJ, or if he had gotten violent with Laurie.

"It would've been better if TJ had told me," he said.

"He was scared."

"Of what?"

"Of you."

Joe frowned at that, like it didn't make sense to him. "It was that he thought he could sit there in rehearsal every day and I wouldn't know. That he didn't respect me enough to tell me right away."

"Fear is different from respect," I said.

A little later, a nurse called his name and he trudged off to get his hand fixed. I just sat and waited, watching the infomercials and the other sad people who came in and waited. Normally I would have been going nuts with boredom by now, but I wasn't. And it was such a relief to be able to sit there not thinking of anything in particular and just wait.

Eventually Joe came back with his hand bandaged up. I got up and stretched. Several joints popped and I wondered how long I had been sitting there.

"Well," said Joe. "Thanks for the ride."

"I'll drive you home," I said.

"You don't have to. I can take the bus."

"It's too late for the bus," I said. "And I want to drive you." I wasn't sure why I did, though.

He looked at me like it was the saddest thing I'd ever said, then he just nodded.

• • •

It only occurred to me while I was following his directions to the Southside that I'd never seen his house. That none of us had. None of us had met his parents. We hadn't even known that he lived in the Southside. It was the worst part of town. Lots of burnt-out, abandoned buildings. If you wanted to buy cheap weed, that's where you went. Otherwise, you stayed away.

Joe lived in the projects. We drove past the identical little apartment buildings that felt more like fortresses than homes. I didn't know how he knew his from any other, but suddenly he said to stop.

He stared straight ahead, his face unreadable as he said, "Thanks for the ride."

Then he got out and walked with slow, measured steps into the building, his chains making a faint *ching ching* sound in the night air.

As I pulled away, somewhere off in the distance, I thought I heard a firecracker. Or a car backfire. Or maybe it was a gunshot.

It was late by the time I got home. Mom had been waiting up for me. Jen5 was with her. They were both sitting at the kitchen table when I walked in.

"Uh . . . hi, guys," I said.

Caring Is Creepy

"Sammy!" they both said, practically in unison. Then they both jumped up and rushed me. Jen5 was ranting about what an asshole Joe was and Mom was going on about how she was getting me a cell phone the very next day.

"Everything's fine," I said.

"Sammy," said my mom, "you really need to think about whether you want this guy as your friend."

"We worked it out," I said. "It's not going to happen again."

"So what actually happened?" demanded Jen5. "Rick was vague as usual on the phone."

I told them everything that had happened. As I was describing it all, I noticed them both looking at me strangely. When I had finished, they looked at each other, then just stared at me some more.

"What?" I said at last.

"What's wrong with you?" asked Jen5.

"What are you talking about?"

"The way you're talking," she said. "It's like you weren't there. Like you're describing a movie."

"Huh?"

"It's not like you," she said. "You're being so cool. So . . . cold."

"Whatever," I said.

"No, not whatever," she said. "What's going on with you? It's like you've turned into Robot Sammy."

"I had a long night," I said. "I'm just tired."

"Ha," she said. "Nice try, but I know you better than that. It's creepy to see you talk like Computer Boy."

"Maybe I'm just tired of feeling so much," I said. "Maybe that's really why I'm tired."

"Oh, so you've just decided you're going to stop giving a shit?"

"Works for everybody else. Why not?"

She didn't reply. Instead, she just looked at her watch. "I gotta go. Let me know when *my* Sammy can come out and play."

Then she walked past me and out of the house.

It dawned on me that my mom had been standing there the whole time, listening to our conversation.

"Well?" I said.

She just shrugged and said, "So if you're tired, go to bed."

"Fine," I said.

I wasn't that tired, and since usually I had to be totally exhausted before I could fall asleep, I decided to work on "Plastic Baby." I had two verses down, so one more and maybe a bridge, and it would be done. I sat on the floor and stared for a long time at what I had written, trying to get myself back into that headspace, that zone. I strummed the rhythm part a little, but nothing came. Everything was all clogged up somewhere inside me. And at the same time, I felt completely empty.

Writer's block.

I tossed my songbook aside and leaned back against my bed. It just wasn't fair. Apparently, I couldn't be a calm, cool, collected guy and still be a songwriter. It was one or the other.

What I needed was a megadose of the Pixies.

The best way to listen to the Pixies is with headphones turned up so that the crash of David Lovering's cymbals, the growl of Kim Deal's bass, and the loudest of Black Francis's screams jab into your ears and hurt just a little. I think they intended just a little pain to go along with it.

I lay on the floor in my room, listening to the Pixies in the prescribed way, letting them rip through "Wave of Mutilation" in my eardrums. If I had to pick my favorite band—and that was kind of unfair because it really depended on my mood— but if I *had* to, it would probably be the Pixies. Usually they filled me with a raging passion that made me want to go out there and really dive into things, no matter how obviously hopeless. Like throwing myself at a tidal wave.

But tonight it was different. I started thinking that here I was, freaking out because my band might be breaking up, when

I knew that the band clearly sucked. I didn't want to break it up, despite the verbal abuse and humiliation, because I just had to be in a band—apparently, any band. I would never be in anything that sounded as good as the Pixies. Listening to their compositions, there were so many parts and rhythm changes that were really surprising, and yet it always sounded exactly right. How did they do that? How did they think of it? Admitting I had no idea made me wonder if I would *ever* know. If I was even capable of knowing. That was especially true of Joey Santiago's guitar work. A lot of people thought he was the weak link in the band. I'd even heard rumors that his dad or uncle or somebody was some rich Cuban druglord who fronted the money to get the band started and that was the only reason he had even been in the band. But those people were totally wrong. I mean, I don't know about the druglord stuff, but it wasn't the only reason he was in the band. Those people just didn't understand what he was doing. They thought his guitar work was simple. And it was. But they remembered it, right? Most of the time, people knew his guitar solos note for note. See, Joey Santiago wasn't just playing the notes. He was playing the silence. Musically speaking, he knew when to shut up. He knew exactly the right thing to say and didn't play a single note more. Now *that* was skill. That was also the depressing part for me. Because I wasn't sure if I could ever be that good. Either musically, or in life.

Gramps said I was like him. Always reaching for the moon.

Maybe that wasn't so bad. When I thought about it, he'd lived a pretty cool life. He had his music and at least he had my grandmother. His one true love. I thought about what he had said, about them being partners in crime and that there wasn't anything they couldn't handle together. What if I never had a girl like that?

Well, there *was* something I could do to improve my chances.

I took the steps two at a time and when I burst into the TV room, my mom glanced up at me from her book, looking completely unsurprised.

"Not tired?" she asked, one eyebrow raised.

"Uh . . . ," I said. "I know it's a school night and all, but I was wondering if maybe I could . . . uh . . . go over to Jen5's . . . just for a little bit."

"On one condition," she said.

"What?"

"That you're going over to apologize."

"Was I really that much of a dick?"

"Yes," she said. "As a matter of fact, you were." Then she turned back to her book, as if I'd already left.

• • •

Fortunately, Jen5 answered the door. I wasn't really in the mood to be polite and reserved with Mr. Russell.

"Hey," she said. She was in sweats and a T-shirt. Her blond hair was wet, like she had just taken a shower, and it almost looked like you could run a comb through it in places. It was weird to see her look so boring and normal. Weird, but kind of cool. Like a peek backstage.

"Hey," I said. "Can we talk a minute?"

She was looking at me suspiciously, her sharp features compressed into something very close to a frown.

"What's up?" she asked as she stepped outside and shut the door behind her.

"I'm sorry," I said. "For being weird tonight. For getting pissed that you were just caring about me. I just . . . I think I was in shock or something."

"Feeling better now?"

"No, I feel like shit now."

"Now, that's my Sammy!" Her face relaxed into a grin, and when I saw that, it was like my chest relaxed at the same time. It was such a relief that I just kept talking.

"Listen, I'm sorry about last night, too," I said.

"Why?" She looked like she had no idea what I was talking about.

Caring Is Creepy

"Uh, well . . ." I wasn't really sure myself what I was talking about. I hadn't ever really figured out what I was sorry about. "Well, you were mad about something I said . . . and then all day today you weren't talking to me, and—"

"Oh . . . ," she said, her eyes softening. "That." She looked down at her toes, scrunched them up on the worn brick stoop. She didn't say anything more.

"What?" I said.

"Look . . . that was just me," she said. She tilted her pale foot to one side and examined the calloused bottom like she was looking for the right words there. "I was mad at myself. I mean, what you said really got me thinking."

"About?"

"Well, you said that I'm never afraid, and that's totally not true at all."

"I know. Sorry, I was exaggerating—"

"Stop apologizing." She finally looked up at me and her paisley eyes gleamed in the white light above the door. "You were totally spot-on. Because I put up this front like I'm never afraid. And that's bullshit. It's not really me. And that's my problem," she said, pressing her hands to her chest. "I don't risk myself enough. You do it all the time. It's one of the things I love about you."

"Do *what* all the time?"

"You walk around with everything out on your sleeve, your chest just this big, gaping wound. I could never do that."

"You don't want to," I said. "Trust me."

"Well, okay," she nodded, "I wouldn't want to do it *all* the time. But I want to be able to do it when I choose." She paused for a second, looking off at nowhere, and pursed her lips for a moment. "I want to be able to do it with you, at least." She paused a little bit longer. "And maybe my dad."

"Your dad?" I hadn't seen that coming.

"Yeah," she said as she looked back at me. Her eyes were a little sad. "I know he's a total freak, but I love him. Someone's got to." A faint flush crept into her cheeks and I could tell that she was trying really hard to do something. Or not to do something. And I thought maybe what she was trying to do was be vulnerable.

"Okay," I said quietly and I took her thin, long-fingered hands in mine. The skin was rough from all the paint she was always scrubbing off them, and probably from sculpture and other art stuff that she did sometimes. I liked the feel of it because it made me less self-conscious of the thick wads of callous on my fingertips from steel guitar strings.

"So maybe we help each other out," I said. "I'll teach you how to be more vulnerable and you'll teach me how to be more of a . . . I don't know . . ." I wasn't sure if she would take "ball-buster" the right way.

Caring Is Creepy

"Kick-ass combat ninja?" she suggested sweetly, leaning in and tilting her head to one side, her eyes half-closed in that way she did when she knew she had me.

"Um," I said. "Not exactly what I was thinking, but I guess we could work with that."

She chuckled quietly and leaned in a little closer. "You're so funny."

"Why am I funny?" I asked, the soft smell of her hair conditioner making it a little hard to think.

Then, with absolutely no warning, she kissed me. I guess it was only fair, since that was what I had done the last time. It started off hard, almost like it was a one-way kiss. But as I wrapped my arms around her narrow shoulders and pulled her in tight, she softened and her breath escaped into my mouth.

"Okay," she whispered after a few minutes. She pulled away. "Parents, just on the other side of this door."

"Oh." My pulse was racing and I couldn't quite catch my breath. "Right."

"Thanks for coming over," she said, then gave me one more quick kiss and slipped back into her house.

"Sure," I said stupidly to the big iron door knocker. "No problem."

Haven't Got a Clue

10

"Joe skipped school today," Rick said as I sat down at the lunch table.

"So?" I said. "He skips all the time."

"Yeah, but . . . ," Rick said. He didn't finish the sentence, but I knew where he was going with it.

"Does Joe even want to be in the band anymore?" asked TJ.

"Do we want to be in a band with him?" asked Rick.

"Yeah," said Alexander. "You guys still doing that Battle of the Bands thing next week?"

"Of course," I said. "Guys, bands go through this kind of stuff all the time. Just give Joe a day or two to cool off and everything will be fine."

They didn't seem very convinced. I couldn't blame them, though, because neither was I.

"Hey," said Rick after a few minutes. "Where's Fiver?"

I shrugged.

"You're supposed to go find her," he said.

"Oh, are you finally giving me some gayfriend advice?" I asked.

"No," he said. "That's what I tell her to do whenever you're hiding under the stairs."

When I needed to get away from stuff, I always headed for some cozy little nook. Jen5 seemed to always look for wide-open spaces. I found her sitting on the curb by the parking lot of the school. She was staring down at some kind of salad thing in a Tupperware container in her lap. She didn't look too thrilled about it.

"Can I sit?" I asked.

"If you can stand the sight of my tofu," she said. "This has to be the most heinous thing to be labeled food since caviar."

"What is tofu, anyway?" I asked.

"Soybean or something," she said.

"It doesn't look much like a bean," I said. "It looks more like chunks of white rubber or something."

"That's about how it tastes, too," she said.

"So what's up?" I asked.

"Nothing."

"Then why are you hiding?"

"I'm not hiding. I'm trying to shield our friends from the hideous sight of my tofu."

"Okay, so how long am I going to have to bug you before you tell me what's really up?"

"Wow, Captain Subtlety strikes again."

"Like you're one to talk. Besides, weren't you just telling me last night you need to be more vulnerable?"

"Okay, okay," she said. She closed her Tupperware container and set it on the asphalt next to us. "So this Saturday, I have a gallery exhibit."

"Your stuff is getting shown somewhere?"

"Yeah." She shrugged.

"Why didn't you tell me about this before?"

"I only found out for sure that it was happening this morning when I checked my e-mail before school. And anyway, it's not really a big deal."

"What do you mean?" I said. "It's a huge deal!"

"Francine is just hanging a bunch of my stuff up at Idiot Child."

"And she's going to have a little opening party or something?"

"Sort of," she said. "See, she and I have been e-mailing back and forth for a while, and—"

"I didn't know that," I said. I thought Francine was more Rick's and my friend.

"Yeah, well, I think she was hoping I was gay or something. I understand. The first time I met her I was wearing a tie, so that probably gave her the wrong idea. Anyway, I made it pretty clear that I was into you, and she said that was the next best thing."

"Wait, I'm the next best thing to being a lesbian?"

"She meant it as a compliment."

"Great," I said. "I'll have to thank her."

"Anyway, so we still kept in touch and she's been really getting into the idea of supporting local artists and stuff. So she wants to start a Saturday night thing, where she exhibits paintings and sculpture and stuff, and also host an open mic."

"An open mic," I said.

"Sam, come on."

"They are the most pretentious, least entertaining thing imaginable. Ninety-nine percent of the people performing at open mics totally and completely suck."

"Which is where you come in," she said.

"What?"

"The other one percent that doesn't suck? That's going to be you."

"Fiver, no!" I jumped up and began to pace. Just thinking about it gave me the creeps.

"Just you and your guitar and a song you wrote."

"I can't do it."

"Please, Sammy."

I was about to go on and on about how I couldn't sing in front of people, but I stopped myself. Because I realized that Jen5's eyes were getting red. In fact, her entire face was getting red. And it looked like she was about to start crying.

"If you won't do it for yourself," she said, "do it for me. Because . . ." She stopped and for a split second, I saw something like fear in her eyes. Then she looked down and stared hard at the lid of her Tupperware container. "Because my mom said she might stop by to check out my stuff, and I'm going to need you to do everything you possibly can to distract me so I don't turn into a total fucking nut."

I stood there and watched her force herself not to cry. I could only take it for about thirty seconds.

"Okay," I said. "I'll sing at the open mic."

"Oh, God, Sammy, thank you!" she said, then jumped up and kissed me hard and gave me a hug. "I know it's a big deal for you," she whispered in my ear. "You really are the best boyfriend ever."

I just stood there in a daze, relieved and horrified all at the same time by what I'd just agreed to.

"It looks like a person, but it's not a person," said Mr. Sully. "So what's the difference? Paint it."

Art class again, a circle of easels around a table. But this time, instead of fruit, it was a statue of some naked Italian guy. No, it was actually a naked Jewish guy (David, I think) but made by some Italian guy.

"This is the worst," groaned Jen5. "Painting a famous statue? Why don't we just make sculptures of the friggin' *Mona Lisa* while we're at it?"

"No fruit, no sculptures," I said. "What *would* you want to paint?"

"Seriously?" she said. "You."

"Ha-ha," I said.

"No, I mean it. Will you model for me?"

"Why would you want to paint me?"

"I've never painted a model," she said. "And I think this falls under the heading of boyfriend duties."

"Does it?"

"Sure." Then she grinned. "I think it would be kind of hot."

"Painting me would be hot?"

She shrugged and gave me a strange look. A look I had never seen before but understood immediately. Or at least, I hoped I did.

"Like . . . how hot?" I ventured.

She shrugged again. There was a mischievous little smirk on her lips.

"My mom has some deposition thing coming up, so she'll be working late all this week," she said. "And my dad has some faculty dinner thing tomorrow night, so . . ."

"Empty house," I said.

"Yep," she said.

"Tomorrow night."

"Uh-huh."

"Well," I said with what I thought was incredible coolness, all things considered, "I just happen to be free for modeling tomorrow night."

"Oh, good," she said. Then she started to paint the statue, but she still had that little smirk while she worked.

I barely paid attention to afternoon classes. There was just too much stuff bouncing around in my head.

Tragedy of Wisdom looked like it might be totally finished. Nobody seemed really desperate to keep it together, except me.

They just didn't see what I saw. What it could be if we just worked a little harder. We'd already put so much into the band. So many nights and weekends of rehearsal, and that wasn't even counting the time I'd spent writing the songs. How could they just shrug all that off? There had to be some way that I could show them what I saw, but I didn't have any ideas.

Then there was the little matter of promising Jen5 that I would sing at an open mic. What was I thinking? Well, you don't tell your crying girlfriend no, is what I was thinking. But the idea made me so queasy, I couldn't really dwell on it too much. But that was okay because there was a third thing that started creeping in and taking over all my other thoughts until it was this huge knot of tension at the back of my head: losing my virginity.

When Jen5 had sort of suggested it in art class, it had been just pure, hot adrenaline rush. But then, as the reality of it started to sink in the rest of the day, I realized that I was terrified. It was just such a mind-boggling thing. Sex. Me. Jen5. In less than forty-eight hours. Holy shit.

I mean, I knew what was supposed to happen. I'd seen my share of porn. But that was just it. The idea of Jen5 actually saying, *Oh, baby! I want your big hard cock!* was just ludicrous. So it clearly wouldn't be like it was in porn. So what, then? I'd seen other movies where it was a lot less in-your-face, but I wasn't sure if that was right either.

And then there were the sex talks I'd had with my mother. She seemed to have this compulsive need to talk to me about the facts of sex. I guess she was just overcompensating because I didn't have a father to talk to me about them. But the stuff she said didn't exactly make me feel any more ready, especially conversations that went something like this:

MOM: You know, Sam, when you do decide to start having sex, which shouldn't be anytime soon because you're much too young—

ME: Oh, God, Mom. Can't we just watch the movie?

MOM: No, I just want to clarify that the scene you have just witnessed has very little to do with a realistic and healthy sexual union.

ME: I get it. It's just a movie. I don't plan on hunting down killer cyborgs, either. Now, can we—

MOM: What you need to remember is that you can't just rush right into intercourse. You have to take your time because a woman needs longer to get into the mood. This is called foreplay.

ME (making strangling noises): Please . . . Mom . . . I'm begging you . . .

MOM: Oh, don't be silly. Now, the reason that it takes longer for a woman is not because she loves

you less or doesn't find you desirable. It's a
physiological thing. In order for her to enjoy
intercourse, her vagina must be lubricated—

ME: Okay, that's it. I'm going to bed.

MOM: Wait, don't you want to know how the movie
ends?

ME: What's the point? I won't be able to hear
what they're saying anyway now that blood
is pouring from my ears.

So, enough of those kinds of talks and you start to feel
this weird pressure. Like you have to do it right or else the girl
won't enjoy it and then you feel like an asshole. And who knew
if the stuff she was telling me was even right. I mean, I think
the last date she went on was when I was ten years old.

So I stumbled from class to class, staring at teachers like I
was paying attention. But all that was in my head was that my
band was breaking up, I was probably going to make an utter
idiot of myself in front of Jen5 in a way that I would never be
able to live down, and then I would follow that up by making
an utter idiot of myself in front of a ton of people at an open
mic. Again.

I felt like I was going to explode if I didn't talk to
someone about it. But pretty much everyone I could talk

to was somehow involved in it. I needed to talk to someone outside the situation.

I parked the Boat in front of Gramps's house after school. The two chairs were still out, and so was the boom box. It was amazing that no one had stolen it. It wasn't a terrible neighborhood or anything, but come on. A little CD player just sitting there? Of course, it had rained the night before, so the thing was probably toast anyway. But it felt weird leaving it there, so I snagged it on my way to the front door.

I knocked. There was no response, but that was normal, so I just opened the door. Immediately, I was hit by the squealing, squawking sounds of a free jazz saxophone solo. Sun Ra? No, it sounded more like Coltrane. I couldn't always tell, because there was never any melody or harmony in free jazz. Just lots of honking, pounding noise.

I peeked in before entering because Gramps didn't listen to free jazz unless he was in a weird mood. The living room was a lot messier than it usually was. Lots of stuff just lying around. Maybe the cleaning person was sick or something. Gramps sat on the hardwood floor in his bathrobe, surrounded by stacks of vinyl records so high, they looked like they could topple over at any second. He was flipping through them quickly, like he was looking for something. Every once in a while, he pulled one out and set it aside, his head nodding and his lips moving a little, like he was talking to himself.

"Hey, Gramps," I said over the screeching saxophone solo.

His head lifted up, and for a just a moment he looked at me in this empty sort of way. Almost how an animal looks at you. Then he gave a flicker of a smile, nodded, and went back to sorting through his albums.

"Whatcha doing?" I asked as I got a little closer.

"Oh, nothing, nothing at all," he said, giving me a sideways glance. Then he was back to his records again. He put the stack down and gathered up all the ones he'd set aside and flipped through them rapidly, like he was shuffling giant cards.

"Um . . . ," I said. "You hungry?"

"Ha!" he said, but didn't look up.

"Well, I am," I said in a way that I hoped was convincing. I actually wasn't very hungry either. "So I'll make us something."

He nodded but continued to shuffle through his albums. I went into the kitchen, grabbed two frozen dinners from the freezer, and popped them into the microwave. The song, which I had finally pegged as Coltrane's "Interstellar Space," squeaked and honked on the stereo while I watched the plastic plates spin around and around. Every once in a while, I could see Gramps's lips move, and one time he actually stopped shuffling, chuckled, and muttered, "Oh really, Johnny?" then went back to flipping through the albums over and over again. This was even weirder than his usual free jazz mood.

I understood the concept of free jazz. Jazz had gone through a lot of changes during the '50s and '60s, and some people felt like it had gotten too formulaic and restricting. Plus, I think that was when the "easy listening" kind of jazz first started to happen, and people were saying that jazz had sold out. So I guess some people like Sun Ra and Coltrane went out to prove that jazz could be just as wild and crazy as it used to be. I appreciated the idea of that, but honestly, listening to it was usually just irritating.

But that night I wondered if it was really as random as it sounded. Was it totally meaningless noise or was there something behind it? Was it even possible that a person like Coltrane, no matter how much junk he'd put in his veins, could ever make pure random noise? Maybe what he was saying was that *everything* was music, even noise, if you knew how to listen to it.

"What's *your* problem?" Gramps's voice was right behind me. I still stood in front of the microwave, even though it had finished cooking. I turned around and saw Gramps scowling at me.

"What do you mean?" I asked. I took our two dinners to the tiny kitchen table and sat down.

He didn't come join me at the table. Instead he just stood by the microwave, his arms folded across his chest, kind of hunched forward. "You're walking around like the weight of the world is on your shoulders. Even more than usual."

"Nothing," I said. He really was in a strange mood, and I wasn't sure now that I wanted to bring up everything that was going on when he was like this.

"Don't bullshit a bullshitter, son. Tell me."

"It's okay," I said. "Really."

"I am old," he said. "I could die at any moment."

"Gramps, please—"

"You want our last interaction to be this? You acting mopey and being generally irritating?"

"Irritating?"

"Damn right," he said. "People who mope are irritating. So spill it."

"Okay," I said. "Fine. My band is breaking up and I have a date tomorrow night that scares the hell out of me."

"Ah." He grinned. "Those sound like my areas of expertise." He took his untouched dish of food from the table and casually tossed it into the sink.

"Aren't you going to eat?" I asked.

"Don't change the subject," he said, then sat down with me. "Okay. First things first. Tell me about the girl."

"Okay," I said. "But you can't tell Mom any of this."

"I probably won't remember tomorrow anyway," he said. "But if there's one thing I know how to do, it's be discreet. Now talk."

"So I'm just nervous is all," I said. "About this date."

"Is this some new girl?"

"No, it's Jennifer. We've been friends forever. We just started dating, though."

"So? If you've known her that long, what do you have to be nervous about?"

"Well, okay . . . See . . . the thing is . . . I think . . . I mean, I don't *know* or anything and I'm not assuming anything, but I think that . . . because her parents won't be at home and stuff . . . I think we're going to have . . . uh . . . sex."

"Ah," he said. Then waited.

"It's . . . uh . . . my first time," I said.

"Oh!" he said. "I get it now. You're worried about that?"

"Yeah."

"Worried how it will go."

"Right."

"Because you don't know what's going to happen."

"Exactly."

He sat there, staring at me and scratching his beard. Then he said, "Sam, sex is like music."

"What?"

"You play by yourself and it sounds okay. But when you play with someone else, that's when the magic happens."

"Okay. . . ." I still wasn't really seeing where this was going.

"It's improvisation," he said. "When you play with someone, you do your thing, but you also listen to their thing. And you try to match it. Try to harmonize. You have to trust what you're doing, but you also have to be open to what they're doing. You just have to listen, Sam. Trust yourself and pay attention. And remember that the first time you play with someone, it's always a little rough. A little awkward. But as long as you play from the heart, you just get better with practice."

I sat there and stared at my untouched plate of food. I didn't know if Gramps was being sane or crazy right then, but he had never talked to me like that before. We sat for a while, not looking at each other, but I felt like there was this whole new channel open between us.

"So," I said finally, "I think my band is breaking up."

He looked at me with a strange expression, like he wasn't exactly sure what I was talking about.

"I got into a fight with the singer of my band."

"Did you win or lose?"

"I guess I won. He had to go to the hospital and I didn't."

"Sounds like a win to me. And so now this joker is sore at you?"

"I guess."

"So get a new band."

"But I can't lead a band."

"Can't or won't?"

"When I have to sing in front of a big crowd, I get so freaked out, I totally freeze up."

"You just have to get over that."

"Gramps, you don't understand how hard it—"

He leaned in really close and poked me in the chest with one bony finger. "You serious about being a musician?"

"Well, yeah."

"You want *easy*, get off this bus right now and go do something practical with your life."

"Gramps, I'm not going to do that. I don't even think I could."

"Then you better realize damn quick that it's never going to be easy. And understand that you made that choice. You. Nobody else."

"But why, Gramps? Why does it have to be hard like that?"

"Because that's an artist's job, Sam. To take this steaming shit pile called life and transform it into something beautiful."

He jerked his head to one side in a weird way, like he was listening to something. He frowned and shook his head.

"You have to risk everything," he said. "Do all the things that scare you, learn from them, and then translate them into something for the world." Then he leaned back in his chair. "They won't appreciate it, of course. Not truly. They'll kiss your ass in that moment because they somehow sense that you're doing something they can't even comprehend, then they'll trade you in for the next hot sound that comes along. Bastards. They're all bastards. But that doesn't matter. You do it because you can't help yourself. Because if you can't make music . . ."

Then suddenly Gramps's head jerked up as if he'd heard a loud noise.

"What now?" he said in a growl, glancing at the pile of records on the floor in the living room.

"What is it, Gramps?" I asked.

His eyes shifted to me, then back to the records, then back to me again.

"Nothing," he said tersely. "Just . . ." He stared at me for a moment, then stood up so suddenly he knocked his chair over. "Just . . ." He looked worried and his hand was in his bathrobe pocket, fiddling with something. "Just, I think you should go."

"Oh . . . ," I said.

"Sorry, kid. You know how it is," he patted me on the shoulder in a "buddy" kind of way. Something he'd never done before. "Got a lot to do. That's all."

"Okay, sure," I said, getting up. It was suddenly like he couldn't wait for me to leave. He practically shoved me to the door.

"Well!" he said with a cheerful voice. "Great seeing you! Tell her hello for me, will you?"

"Her who?" I asked. Did he mean Jen5? My mother?

"Oh!" he said, and gave a forced laugh. "I think you know who I mean!" But he said it in a way that made me question whether *he* knew what he meant.

"Yeah, you bet," I said, and let him push me out the door. "Good—"

The door slammed closed.

"I'm getting worried about Gramps," I said to Jen5 that night on the phone.

"Yeah?" she asked. "Well, he's pretty old, Sammy. And it's not like he ever really took care of himself, you know?"

"I know," I said. "It's just . . . sometimes he's so cool, and then the next minute, he acts like somebody I don't even know. Mom said something about looking at nursing homes the other day. You think he's losing it?"

"My grandma is in a home," she said. "She loves being there. All her little bingo friends and stuff. She says it was the best thing for her. Maybe it would be like that for him. Maybe he'd be happier in a home."

"Maybe," I said, although it really didn't sound like Gramps's style.

"Samuel Bojar!" my mother called from downstairs. "Are you talking on the phone when you should be doing your homework?"

Damn that little green light.

"Of course not!" I called down to her. Then on the phone: "Gotta go."

"Oh, real quick," said Jen5.

"Yeah?" I said.

"Don't forget to . . . uh . . . go to the *drugstore* before you come over for our modeling session tomorrow."

"Oh," I said. Then I realized what she was talking about. "Oh! Yeah, of—of course . . ."

"Sweet dreams." Then she hung up.

Condoms. I had just officially been asked to purchase condoms.

It took forever to fall asleep that night.

Yerself Is Steam

11

There were so many kinds of condoms.

The school day had taken forever to get through, although I couldn't really remember anything that happened. It had all been a blur of anticipation even more intense than waiting for a concert. But finally the last bell rang.

And now I stood in the back aisle of the drugstore and stared at the wall of condoms like they were in a foreign language. Ribbed, lubricated, ultrathin, sensitive, lambskin, flavored, glow-in-the-dark . . . I didn't even know what half of those meant. And there were sizes, too. Jesus, I didn't know what *size* I needed. I stood paralyzed for a full ten minutes as I stared at the many colored boxes that hung in front of me.

Why was buying condoms so embarrassing? It wasn't like

there was something to be ashamed of, right? If anything, I should be able to walk up to the register and proudly place them on the counter and say, *Yes, I'm going to get laid tonight! And since I am a responsible person, I plan to use a condom!* So why could I already feel a slow blush creeping into my face? Why was I tempted to actually steal them just so I didn't have to take them to the counter? Honestly, the only thing that stopped me from swiping them was the possibility of an even worse embarrassment: being caught shoplifting condoms. I could picture being held back in the manager's office until my mom showed up and I had to tell her. I couldn't imagine anything worse than that.

But I couldn't just stand there and stare at them forever, either. So I took a deep breath, grabbed the one that seemed the most standard, and headed to the counter.

There was some old lady at the register. Of course. It *had* to be an old lady. I tried to place them on the counter confidently. Like it was no big deal. But I think my hand might have been shaking a little. And my face was so hot, I'm sure it was beet red.

The lady was used to this kind of thing, though. She didn't even blink. Just scanned them and told me how much they were and I paid.

"Thanks," I said. My voice was shaking a little too.

. . .

As I drove over to Jen5's house, I suddenly remembered the "real" reason I was coming over. I was supposed to be her model. The idea of being a model seemed a little strange, but I knew she preferred to paint portraits and still lifes from living things, and I guess if you wanted to paint a real person, it would be weird to ask someone you didn't know and almost as weird to ask someone you did know. I guess asking your boyfriend was probably the least weird. And while I'd never tried to sit completely still for an hour or two, how hard could it be?

When I pulled up at Jen5's house, she was already waiting for me, just sitting on the front stoop. She was wearing her painting gear, which was overalls and a tube top. On anyone else it might have looked trashy, but somehow on her it transformed into some kind of funky, dirty artist look. At her feet, she had a boom box.

"You ready to be immortalized?" she asked as I climbed out of the Boat.

"As I'll ever be," I said. "What's with the stereo?"

"Entertainment for you," she said. "This could take a while."

"Could?" I asked.

"Yeah, well, I never know. I don't plan anything ahead of

time. Like, I purposely don't. So this could be a simple little sketch or it could be a five-hour painting marathon."

"Five hours?" I said.

"Don't worry, I'll let you take breaks. Now, come on. Let's get started."

We walked back behind her house to her studio, which was an old wooden shed. Her dad wasn't really into yard work or home improvement, so it had just sat empty until Jen5 asked her parents if she could convert it into a studio. It was a small rectangular space, with bare wood floor and walls. All of her art supplies were on shelves on one side, and a big white canvas backdrop was on the other. It was a little stuffy and there weren't any windows, so she had to a run an air filter all the time to clear out the paint fumes. But it was her own space where she could work in complete privacy with her CD player blaring and everything just the way she wanted it.

As soon as we got inside, she said, "Take your shirt off."

Then she went over and started mixing paints.

I felt vulnerable as I took my shirt off, especially the way she just commanded it to happen. I was kind of a skinny guy and always felt even skinnier when I was shirtless. Of course, it wasn't like Jen5 had never seen me with my shirt off before. We'd gone swimming tons of times over the years. But things were a lot different now. Obviously. And Jen5 was totally in painter mode. She was so focused on setting up the equipment and everything that it almost didn't even feel like her.

"Sit on that stool," she said while she set up her palette and a canvas.

I sat down, but that didn't help my nerves. If anything, I felt even more like some kind of specimen to be examined.

She came over and adjusted the folds in the backdrop behind me.

"You're nervous," she said.

"I guess," I admitted. "I just don't know what to do."

"You don't have to do anything," she said.

"Yeah, that's the problem. I like having something to do."

"Here," she said. Then she switched on the boom box and a mellow, spacey jam started playing.

"Mercury Rev?" I asked.

"Huh?" she said. She was back to fixing the backdrop and adjusting the clip lights that hung from the ceiling.

"The song," I said. "It's Mercury Rev. I didn't know you liked them."

"Oh, I don't know. It's some mix you made me a few years ago. When you were trying to get me out of my classical music groove."

"Oh, right," I said. "I remember that."

I listened to the song as she continued to set things up.

"Car Wash Hair," one of my all-time favorites. It had the feeling of a lazy summer, both sad and happy at once.

"Mixes are funny," I said.

"How's that?" She was still messing with some kind of lighting thing.

"Well, you pick songs, you know, and most of the time you aren't really thinking about why. You're just thinking about that person and then thinking, 'Oh, this would sound great next.' But maybe there's some kind of subconscious thing at work. I mean, this song . . . then I think there's that Cure song, 'Just Like Heaven.' Then that Pixies song, 'La La Love You.' And I think there's even a Magic Numbers song in there . . . I mean, come on."

"I can't believe you remember what you put on a mix you made me two years ago."

"But that's exactly it," I said. "All that thought I put into it. Didn't I see that I was making you a crush mix?"

She shrugged. "I don't know. I thought it was pretty obvious."

"It's like we do all these things and don't know why we do them, and then we look back and it's like, 'Of course! That's why I did it!' I don't know . . . I mean, I wonder if I'll ever be able to see the reason for things while I'm actually doing them. You know?"

"Yeah . . . ," she said. Then she looked at me with a weird sort of half-smile.

"Should I be posing now?" I said. "Are you, like, thinking about the painting or something?"

"I am," she said. "But don't start posing." She picked up her palette and brush, walked over to me. Then she reached out with her brush and drew a line on my shoulder.

I moved away a little. "What are you doing? I thought you were going to paint me."

She still had that half-smile. "I am. Come here. Get closer." Her eyes were different, somehow. Really open wide. "Trust me."

I leaned back in, not sure what the hell was going on at all.

"Thanks," she said. Then she took her brush and drew a long slow line of red from my shoulder to my wrist. It felt strange. Wet and cool and really, really soft. It made me shiver a little.

"Is this . . . ," I said. "Is this . . ."

"Shhh," she said, and tapped the paintbrush on my lips. Then she lightly drew a circle around my mouth. She was close now. So close I could smell her. Her own mixture of hair product and paint. I could feel heat coming off of her skin. I could see her pulse beating in her neck. I stared at her eyes, those paisley eyes that you could trip out on like the visualizations on MP3 players. And I could feel the brush trace from the corner of my mouth, along my jawline, down my neck, and onto my chest. My brain started to flip out on me. It was all too much to take in at once. There could have been sparks coming from my ears and I wouldn't have been surprised. Her breath was on my skin and her smell was in my head, and I could feel heat— real heat—coming off of her body, and that Mercury Rev song was still playing and all the while that soft brush moved up and down my chest, my arms, my stomach. I was going nuts. I didn't want it to end. But I couldn't help myself. I grabbed her by her overalls and pulled her into a kiss. Paint from my face smeared on hers. I could feel her bare, sweating shoulders in my hands. Her fingers were in my hair and she sighed into my ear.

Then I heard a *ping ping* as I popped the clasps off her overalls. And then I melted and she melted, or at least that's how it seemed to me because the only thing in my brain was heat.

It was our first duet.

As I drove home that night, something was different. I felt like electricity tingled beneath my skin. Sure, some of it was the dried paint on my arms and chest. But the rest of it was something I couldn't quite get a handle on. Like what Gramps was always talking about, some kind of magic or mystery. There are those guys that pretend that it's not a big deal. But those guys are either lying assholes or soulless robots from another planet.

Because that first time is so crazy and cool and kind of intensely embarrassing that it might be the biggest deal in your life so far. Nothing prepares you for it. Not movies or books or your friends talking about it. Definitely not your mother. I could see how if it wasn't with someone you could trust, if you were really worried the girl might laugh at you if you did something wrong, I could see how that could make it the biggest mind-fuck of your life. But I did trust Jen5. There probably wasn't another person alive that I trusted more. And Gramps was right. You didn't really worry about what to do, any more than you worried about what note comes next in an improv. Your brain was on a deeper level.

When I got home, Mom was in bed, but waiting up for me. When I kissed her good night, she said, "Is that paint on your face?"

I'd thought I'd gotten most of it off my face, but I guess not enough.

"Yeah," I said. "Jen5 was doing some art thing."

"Painting people?" she asked.

I shrugged. "I didn't really understand it either. But if I don't do that kind of weird stuff for her, who will?"

She gave me a look that I couldn't quite understand, and I thought there might be more interrogation. But then she just said, "All right. Good night, Sam. Take a shower before you go to bed. I don't want you getting paint on your sheets."

Yerself Is Steam

· · ·

Everyone lies to their parents about something. You learn pretty quick that no matter what they say, parents don't really want to know everything. When you were a kid, they shielded you (or tried to anyway) from stuff like death and poverty and disease. So now you protected your parents. You shielded them from the knowledge of how close you came to getting sucked into drugs and sex and craziness in one way or another. Because really, they didn't want to know. It would drive them so crazy, they would probably either lock you in a room and have you homeschooled by a nun or else they'd move the family to Montana or someplace where life hadn't changed in fifty years. If there even were places like that anymore. And it wasn't like they hadn't done half of those things themselves. But what they couldn't handle was *you* doing them.

So I was used to lying to Mom a little and it usually only bothered me a little. But lying about my relationship with Jen5 really bugged me. It made me feel like I was doing something wrong. But I wasn't this time. It was one of the few things in my life I was sure about, but I also knew that when I told Mom, she would totally flip out.

But even that couldn't get me down. I was feeling too good. I didn't mind the buzzing slot machine of my mind while I lay in bed. Mainly it was just images of Jen5.

12

I woke up late and happy, but then
I spent Saturday morning stressing about what song I was
going to play for the open mic that night. I wished I could
do "Plastic Baby," but it still needed at least one more verse,
and I wasn't quite sure where I was going with it yet. So I
went through a bunch of others, some that we'd been working
on in Tragedy of Wisdom, some that had been sitting in my
songbook because I knew they weren't the kind of songs Joe
would want to do. Eventually, I decided on a upbeat little song
called "Postmarked Super Queen" about this girl that I dated
for a few months freshman year who broke up with me in a
letter. It was a goofy, fun song that I hoped would make the
whole open mic experience less painful. Maybe if I just kept it
light, I'd be able to get through it.

I went over to Jen5's place at four. The open mic didn't start until eight, but she wanted to get there early to help Francine set up.

She answered the door and gave me a quick kiss. "Hey, I'm running a little late. I still have to get dressed."

I looked at her. She was wearing a T-shirt and jeans. "You look fine," I said.

"Thanks, but I want to dress up a little for this," she said.

"Dress up? What, like a gown or something?"

"Like hell," she said. "No, just stuff that's a little nicer than what I normally wear. You know. Stuff I don't want to mess up."

I had no idea what that stuff might be, but I was really interested to see it. "Okay," I said.

"So maybe you can just hang out for a little while."

"Sure," I said.

I didn't realize that meant hanging out with her dad. But a little bit later, there I was, sitting in the big cold study in a high-backed, uncomfortable antique chair trying like hell to make conversation with Mr. Russell. I hadn't talked to him since Jen5 and I had started dating, and the vibe was completely different. He wasn't just my friend's father anymore. Now he was my *girlfriend's* father.

"Samuel," he said. He sat in a different uncomfortable antique chair with his hands carefully folded in his lap.

"Good to see you, Mr. Russell," I said. My palms were already sweating.

"It is my understanding," said Mr. Russell, "that the nature of your relationship with my daughter has changed."

"Um," I said, "that's right."

"Don't say 'um,'" said Mr. Russell. "It makes you sound doltish and ill-mannered."

"Sorry," I said.

"While humility is admirable," said Mr. Russell, "apologizing for an accidental mistake is pointless and suggests a weakness of character. Had you known your error, then an apology would have been appropriate. In the case of being informed of an error of which you were ignorant, an apology is academic."

"Thank you," I said, not knowing what else to say. I was already totally flunking the interview.

"Samuel, you agree that your relationship with Jennifer has changed," said Mr. Russell. "In what way would you say it has changed?"

"That's kinda complicated," I said.

"Inevitably," he said. "Do your best to summarize."

"Well, in a lot of ways, things are the same. I mean, we're still best friends and all. But everything's more . . . intense, you know? I mean, you think that friendships are intense, right? But then this is like ten times that. Like sometimes it's so much that it just blows your mind. Like something you never knew you were missing but now that you have it, you can't imagine life without it."

I eyed him uneasily. I didn't even think *I'd* followed that.

"I see," was all he said. We sat there in total silence for a long time. I could hear an old clock ticking off in the distance and I wondered how Jen5 could be taking so long to get ready.

"So, Samuel," Mr. Russell said at last. "You are a musician, correct?"

"Yes, sir," I said.

"And guitar is your instrument?"

"Mainly, sir."

"You play other instruments?"

Normally I didn't tell people this, because it sounded kind of conceited and nerdy. But I thought Mr. Russell might appreciate it. "Well," I said, "I actually started on trumpet. My grandfather is a jazz musician, and he's really into Miles Davis. So he got me my first horn when I was in third grade."

"Your grandfather is a musician?"

"He's retired now, but yeah."

"Locally?"

"I guess he really got his break up in Detroit and Cleveland and moved down here with my mom after my grandmother died."

"Forgive me," said Mr. Russell. Underneath his normal glare, he suddenly seemed kind of excited. "I must ask. Is your grandfather Jack Bojar?"

"Yeah." I was kind of surprised that he knew him. "Yeah, he is."

Mr. Russell leaned back in his seat and smiled. "I'd always wondered why your last name seemed familiar to me. I'm sure you know, your grandfather is one of the greatest pianists of the bop era to come out of this region."

"Well, thanks, Mr. Russell," I said. "I know he'll be really glad to hear that."

"Will you tell him?"

"Of course," I said. "He's . . . Well, he could really use some compliments like that right now. Things aren't really that . . . easy for him anymore."

Mr. Russell was acting really weird now. He kept nodding his head and rubbing his hands together. "I have a recording. You might know it. The Newport Jazz Festival in 1966. I was a student in Rhode Island at the time. I must confess that my interest in jazz was minimal. But a friend of mine convinced me to go with him. It was a pivotal moment in my life. It was where I developed a true love for modern jazz. I witnessed your grandfather play an extended solo improvisation of 'Stormy Weather' by Harold Arlen and Ted Koehler, and in that moment, I understood, for the first time, the possibilities of the form. It was then that I realized that jazz was not simply popular dance music. It had been elevated to a noble artistic form." Then he suddenly stood up. "If you haven't heard it, I'd be pleased to play it for you."

"Yeah," I said, kind of stunned. "That'd be great." I'd never heard a recording with Gramps. He was mainly a live performance musician, someone who sat in with whoever was coming through town. That was back when you could do that and make a living without ever really putting out an album of your own. He'd told me he was on lots of other people's albums, as a fill-in studio musician, but that most of those albums were impossible to find or else just total crap.

Mr. Russell walked quickly over to a big wooden closet. I saw his hands shake a little as he reached for the handles, and the expression in his eyes was just like when Rick got a new Xbox game. Jen5's dad was totally geeking out on jazz right in front of my eyes. He opened the closet and on the inside was a huge mahogany frame with speakers and a record player inset. He slid open a drawer at the bottom that was packed tightly with records. It looked like they were in alphabetical order, and he flipped through them quickly until he pulled one out. The album cover was a picture of either a sunrise or a sunset (I couldn't tell which) and just had the words *Newport*

Jazz Festival, Live, 1966. He carefully slid the record out of the sleeve and placed it on the turntable. I could tell he knew exactly what he was looking for, because he counted the lines and set the needle down about halfway through the record.

Right away, a drum-and-upright-bass combo kicked in over the speakers, pretty much just a mellow, cool vamping groove. Something to give the soloist room to do whatever he wanted. Then a piano came crashing in and I knew immediately it was Gramps. His playing style was as familiar to me as his voice. But I never heard him play like this. So free and wild, but you knew that every note was on purpose. One moment it sounded like he was pounding those keys so hard he would break his fingers, then he would slide into some smooth, ultracool riff that just sent shivers down your back.

I don't know how long we listened, but Mr. Russell and I were still standing there with music washing over us when I heard Jen5 behind me. "Dad, are you forcing your record collection on my boyfriend?"

I turned to her and I think I might have been getting a little teary all of a sudden as I said, "It's my grandfather. He has my grandfather on record."

Jen5's mouth opened wide and she stared back and forth between me and her dad.

"Oh," was all she could say. "Wow."

Taste the Pain

And then, with Gramps's music still crashing in my ears, I looked at Jen5. Really looked. She had carefully twisted up her dreadlocks and tied them in chunks with bits of old lace and ribbon. She'd put on eye shadow or something that brightened the kaleidoscopic colors of her eyes. She had on some kind of tight lacy tank-top thing that looked more like lingerie than anything, and over that was a fitted red satin suit coat. And she wore a skirt, or maybe a black canvas kilt, all ragged and torn, with safety pins glittering everywhere. To finish it all off, she had on knee-high chunky black boots.

"Wow," I said, like an echo of her. "Fiver, you look . . . unbelievable."

She gave me a sly grin and winked.

"I clean up pretty good, huh?" she said.

"Well," Mr. Russell said absently, still staring at the record, still zoned into Gramps's piano. "You clean up *well*."

Jen5 and I showed up at Idiot Child around six. It was weird seeing the place during the day and before the cigarette smoke and the smell of dirty punks and hippies had time to fill it up. I had never noticed that there were big bay windows up front. The late-afternoon sunlight shone in through them and lit the place up all warm and happy, with little bits of dust floating around. It was almost like some enchanted fairyland. But, you know, with old couches and graffiti and stuff. It was so bright and fresh that when Jen5 and I first stepped through the door, I thought we'd somehow come into the wrong place. That is, until I heard a harsh female voice say, "Sammy Bojar, I don't give a shit if you're happy to see me or not, but that better be a guitar you're holding."

"Hi, Francine," I said.

She was over in the far corner, where she had cleared away the furniture to make room for a tiny, four-foot-wide platform. She was setting up a sound system with a mic and stand. She was pretty big, like I said before, but a lot of that was muscle. She was wearing a black tank top and her tattooed arms flexed and strained as she shoved an amp and speaker stack back behind the little platform. She had a cigarette dangling from the corner of her mouth as she talked. Once she had admitted to me that it took a lot of practice to master that.

"You *are* playing tonight, right?" she asked.

"I don't think I have a choice," I said. "By the way, thanks for saying that I was the next best thing to being a lesbian."

"Hey," said Francine. "If I were ever to go back to boys, you'd be top on my list. Anyway, the both of you are on the house tab tonight. Hey, Raef!"

Raef's head popped up from behind the counter. "Yo, Franny!" he said.

"Any luck with that signal of yours?"

He sighed and shook his head. "So close, Franny. So close."

"Well, Jen5 and Sammy get free coffee all night. The fancy stuff, if they want it."

"Cool," said Raef. Then he looked at us. "Mochas? Lattes? What's your flavor? I make a mean double con panna . . ."

"Straight espresso for me," said Jen5. "I'm going to need it."

"How about you, Sammy?"

"Just water until after I play," I said. It sucked, but I knew I'd be nervous enough without the caffeine.

Raef shrugged. "Suit yourself."

"Okay," said Francine. "Now that's settled, Sammy, put your stuff down and come help me with this goddamn sound system."

Setting up took a lot longer than it needed to. Mainly because the acoustics of the place were terrible and Francine was picky. I must have stood in front of that mic saying, "Testing, one, two, three," for an hour while she ran all over the shop, listening, puffing on her cigarettes, swearing under her breath, and instructing me to bring up the reverb or bring down the bass. I knew it wasn't doing much because there wasn't much that could be done with a single mic and a cheap amp. But it seemed to make Francine happy, in her gruff, angry kind of way, and it got me some time to get used to being at the mic. I knew it would all change once the people were in there, but it was better than nothing.

Jen5 was doing the same kind of pointless activity with her paintings. She would tilt the frame a little one way, step back, cock her head to the side, then move it back where it was before.

Once we finished with our pointless sound check, I walked around and looked at all the paintings. Jen5 sat in a chair and I could feel her eyes following me. She was probably fighting the urge to trail behind me, which I appreciated. It's awkward to try to check out someone's artwork while they breathe down your neck the whole time.

A lot of the paintings I'd seen before, at her house. When Jen5 was painting for fun and not for some assignment, the energy was still there, like the colors had been beaten on the canvas with a club. But these were darker, more private. It was Jen5 without the sarcasm. Without the shield. I wondered if she realized that the vulnerability she had such a hard time showing in real life was on every canvas.

Then I saw a painting that I'd never seen before. It was a portrait of me. Not taken from life, obviously, since we'd never gotten around to that, but from memory. As she saw me in her head. It's hard to describe how it feels to see something like that.

And how different it looks from your own self-image. In the picture, I was just standing there with my hands in my pockets. The edges were blurred, like I was emerging from the chaotic darkness in the background. Or fading *into* the chaos. It was hard to tell. I looked gaunt and hungry, kind of like a starved wolf. And I was staring up at a distant, dirty yellow crescent moon.

"That's my favorite," Francine said from over by the counter.

"It doesn't have a price marked," I said. "The rest of them have a little tag in the corner with the title and price."

"It's not for sale," said Jen5. "I just wanted to show it."

There's times when you feel so intensely about something or someone that you don't know what to do or how to say it without it sounding cheesy. There's times when real communication is just impossible because you'd need to invent a whole new language to describe how you feel. Words like "happy" and "sad" only make it more obvious how impossible it all is. That was how it was right then. I stared at Jen5. She sat in a chair and looked back at me, probably trying to figure out if I liked the painting or not. But "like" didn't really even make sense. It was a useless word. The painting *moved* me. See? It sounds cheesy. So I said nothing. But I couldn't just leave her hanging. I knew that. So I walked over to her, tilted her chin up with my fingertips, leaned over, and kissed her.

Maybe I was thinking it would be a nice, sweet, gentle kiss. But when my lips touched her, it was like she exploded. Her hand grabbed a fistful of my hair and she pressed her mouth against mine so hard it almost hurt. Almost. Funny how "almost hurt" can feel so good.

"God! Get a hotel room!"

Jen5 and I looked up and saw Rick walking through the front door.

"What are you doing here?" I asked.

"You're kidding, right?" he said. "How could I miss a double bill of Jen5 and Sammy Bojar?"

"I'm only playing one song," I said. "It's mostly going to be a lot of people doing poetry and spoken word."

"Well." Rick shrugged. "I'd probably be hanging out here anyway. Where else would I go?"

"What about a club?" said Francine. "Isn't that where all the gay boys go?"

"Only if they dance," said Rick. He usually didn't like being called a gay boy or even really talking about being gay very often. But for some reason, maybe because she was gay, Francine could talk about it as much as she wanted and it didn't seem to bother him. He turned to Raef, "Hey, dude. Set me up with a tall hot one."

"See," said Francine, "you have to go to a club to find one

of those. But I'll have a look around tonight and see if there's anyone I can introduce you to."

"That's not even a little funny," said Rick. "We talked about this. I'm not in the meat market."

"Fine, fine," said Francine. "By the way, I'll give you free coffee if you work the door tonight."

"I didn't think you were charging a cover," said Jen5.

"I'm not," said Francine. "I just realized I should collect some e-mail addresses for a newsletter or something. You know, I really want to make this into a regular thing. Plus, it might make people feel better if there's a bouncer-looking person there."

"Free mochas all night?" said Rick. "Just to collect some contacts and look tough?"

"*Try* to look tough," said Jen5.

We all settled into place. Rick sat by the door with a notepad. He was wearing one of Francine's baseball caps because he said that would make him look more like a bouncer. I thought it actually made him look more like a frat boy, but I didn't say anything because he seemed to be having fun. Francine and Raef were both behind the counter, which only happened when they expected to be really busy. Jen5 and I sat on a couch in the corner, trying not to stare at everyone who came in.

First it was just a trickle, mainly regulars who had no idea there was even anything going on. Jen5 was nervous, and it looked like Francine was too. They were probably worried that no one would show. I wanted there to be a lot of people for them, but there was a part of me that hoped the crowd would be small. I was still pretty sure I'd freeze when I got up there to sing, so I thought it would be best if as few people as possible saw my public humiliation. My hopes were crushed around seven thirty, though, when it seemed half the underground scene in Columbus piled in at once. Everyone was checking out Jen5's stuff and it wasn't long before she started getting antsy.

"Screw this," she said and jumped to her feet. "I'm going to hover."

A moment later, she was weaving in and out of the clusters of hipsters, hippies, punks, skaters, and goths. That left me alone, which was fine. I didn't feel much like talking anyway. There was this ball of ice in my stomach. I found myself wishing that there were even *more* smokers than usual; maybe if everyone in the room started puffing, the smoke would get so thick that I couldn't see the audience. Because that was the only way I was going to be able to do this.

I don't know how long I sat there slowly sinking into terror, but eventually Jen5 came back.

"Hey," she said as she sat down next to me.

"How'd it go?" I managed to force out.

"Great," she said. "I already sold two pieces. Can you believe it?"

"You're kidding," I said, hoping there was enthusiasm in my voice. "That's awesome." I really wanted to be excited for her, but the dread was weighing me down so much I felt like I could barely breathe.

"What's wrong?" she asked. "Are you feeling okay? You look kind of pale."

"Can I just do an instrumental?" I asked.

"No way," she said. "You promised."

I nodded. I had promised. And anyway, as soon as I'd said it, I remembered Gramps poking me in the chest and demanding to know if I was serious about being a musician. Even though he wasn't there, this was how I could prove that I was serious. At least to myself.

Then the open mic began. Francine was a pretty good emcee. She was funny and everyone knew who she was. She gave everyone two minutes, more or less. She wouldn't cut someone off or anything, but if you didn't give some kind of limit, people would just go on forever. Like this girl Melissa that I sort of knew. She had a shaved head except for one purple lock and always wore ripped fishnet thigh-highs that were way too small for her. Anyway, she was one of the first people up there. She busted into some spoken-word thing that started, "I am not a used condom you can flush down the toilet of your life."

And people wondered why I hated open mics. It was mostly stuff like that. Goofy, recycled, angsty bullshit. One after another, they got up and rattled off their "outsider" rant, or their "secretly suffering on the inside" rant, or the ever-popular "I just got my heart broken and I'm thinking about killing myself" rant.

There was one guy who got up there, though, who I'd never seen before. He looked a little drunk, but he was kind of funny: "I met this girl and she was rich and pretty and she had a WHITE JEEP!!! We started dating and we had a good time and I screwed her in the WHITE JEEP!!! But then one day she got robbed. She was spending the night at my place and someone stole her WHITE JEEP!!! We broke up soon after that because I realized that I didn't really like that rich pretty girl. I liked—I loved—the WHITE JEEP!!!"

I don't know why, but that cracked me up. And it was nice to be distracted from my impending doom.

We were listening to some pimply dude in a black trenchcoat mutter about becoming a vampire when I suddenly felt Jen5 tense up next to me.

Taste the Pain

"What's wrong?" I whispered.

"Mrs. Russell has arrived," she hissed, and there was a lot of conflict in her voice. Anger but also a kind of longing. And underneath, fear.

Mrs. Russell stood in the doorway, her nose wrinkled as she looked around at the big room of troubled teenagers. Her blond hair was pulled back in a tight bun that made her sharp features look even more angular. She wore some dark blue lawyer power suit and still held on to her laptop bag. I don't think anyone in the world would have stuck out more. Even Mr. Russell, who stood a little bit behind her in his powder-blue polo shirt and neatly combed gray hair, looked less out of place.

Rick, who was still sitting by the door, leaned over and said something to Mrs. Russell, probably something smart-ass, by the look on his face. He and Mrs. Russell had never gotten along. She looked down at him, her nose still scrunched up, but didn't reply to whatever he said.

"Come on," whispered Jen5. "Let's go over there before Rick pisses her off."

We weaved our way through the crowds to the door.

"Hi, Mom," said Jen5.

"Jennifer." Mrs. Russell nodded curtly.

"Hey, Dad," she said, and gave him a quick hug.

"Hi, Mr. and Mrs. Russell," I said.

"Samuel," said Mrs. Russell. Mr. Russell just nodded and gave me a tight smile. When Mrs. Russell was around, he hardly ever spoke.

"It's going great, Mom," said Jen5. "I've already sold two pieces."

"How much?" said Mrs. Russell.

"What?" said Jen5. "Uh, twenty-five each."

"Why so little?"

"Well, they only cost me a couple of bucks in supplies."

"But your *time*, Jennifer," said Mrs. Russell. "Time is your most precious commodity."

"Okay," she said in a meek voice.

"Glad you could come, Mr. and Mrs. Russell," I said, making a point to bring Mr. Russell into the conversation. It bothered me how Jen5 and her mom talked to each other like he wasn't even there. "This is only the first one Francine's had and we've got a huge crowd."

"I hear you'll be performing this evening," said Mrs. Russell. "Up there." She pointed with her chin at the tiny platform stage where some hippie dude was going on about how we were slowly killing the earth with pesticides.

"Yes, ma'am," I said. "Jennifer talked me into it."

Mrs. Russell's mouth curled up a little at the edges, which

I think was supposed to look like a smile. For reasons I could never understand, Mrs. Russell had always liked me. Not that she was nice to me or anything, but she always seemed to make an effort to smile at me.

"Are you going to stick around for a little while, Mrs. Russell?" asked Rick.

"No," she said. "I have to get back to the office."

Rick said, "At nine o'clock on a Saturday?"

Mrs. Russell looked down at him and said, "Imagine that."

"Aren't you going to look around at my stuff?" asked Jen5.

"The smoke in this place is disgusting." Her mouth curled down at the ends, which for most people was a frown, but for her was just normal. "Really, Jennifer. I hope this artist phase of yours is over soon. You're so much better than this." She turned to Mr. Russell, who seemed to be totally absorbed in the hippie guy's poem. "Jeffrey?"

"What?" he said, blinking like he was snapping out of a trance.

"Time to go," she said.

"Ah," he said. Then he turned and nodded to us, an apologetic smile on his face. "Sorry we couldn't stay longer. It looks lovely, Jennifer, and we're both very proud of you. Samuel, I'm sure you'll sound wonderful. And Richard . . . well, I'm sure you have contributed greatly to the security of this event." Then he nodded curtly and looked to Mrs. Russell to lead the way.

Mrs. Russell turned to go.

"Mom," said Jen5. There was a weird shaking in her voice. Like she wanted to yell or cry or maybe tell her dad to get a backbone or maybe her mother to go to hell. But instead, she said, "Thanks for coming."

Mrs. Russell shrugged. "For what it's worth." Then she turned and left.

Jen5 stood and stared at the empty doorway. A muscle in her jaw twitched.

"Come here," I said, pulling her to me.

She stiffened and resisted. "I'm fine."

"I know," I said, and kept pulling her closer.

"I don't need comforting," she said.

"Of course," I said, wrapped my arms around her.

"It's just my mom," she said, but she started leaning into me.

"You're right," I said. "I just wanted a hug."

"Okay," she sighed. She sank into my arms until her shoulder was against my chest and her head rested on my shoulder.

I don't know how long we stood like that in the back of Idiot Child. Long enough for me to lose track. I usually wasn't into public displays of affection, but right then it was almost as if I forgot we were even in public. It was just the smell of her hair and the feel of her ribs expanding and contracting with breath beneath my hands. I thought about our conversation a few nights ago, about teaching each other strength and vulnerability. A couple of weeks ago, she would never have rested her head on *anybody's* shoulder, especially not in public. Maybe that meant it was working—teaching each other things, making each other better people.

But then a voice cut into my thoughts. A harsh female voice that said, "And last but not least, to close out Idiot Child's first ever open mic, is a good friend and great musician, Sammy Bojar."

Now it was my turn to stiffen up.

"Go on," whispered Jen5. "Sing me a song." Then she pushed me toward the stage.

That walk through the crowd was how I imagined a walk down death row would feel. I sure felt like I was about to die, anyway. My knees locked up and I couldn't walk naturally, like I had forgotten how. I just barely remembered to grab my guitar from where I had been sitting, then shuffled the rest of the way up onto the platform. I sat down on a little stool and adjusted the mic.

"Umm," I said, then looked out at the audience. It

wasn't that they looked hostile or anything. But they weren't exactly smiling, either, and there were about fifty of them. Fifty people who either knew me or knew someone who knew me and were probably thinking the exact same thing that I thought every time someone got up at an open mic, which was *Oh, God, here's another wannabe singer-songwriter.* I got dizzy and I suddenly felt cold and my vision was blurry. I thought I was going to pass out right there. There was no way I could do this. No way I could even talk, much less sing. My eyes bounced around at all the people sitting there staring up at me. They wouldn't like it. How could they possibly like it?

But then I saw Jen5 all the way in the back by the door. Her arms were wrapped around her torso and she was kind of leaning to one side so that one of her blond dreadlocks fell across her face. Seeing her there in that kilt-and-boots thing, she just looked so hot and sad all at once that I wanted to say forget it, grab her, and take off. But I couldn't do that, because she'd asked me to sing her a song.

Couldn't it be just as simple as that? Screw the rest of these people. I hardly knew them. They didn't even matter. I was just going to sing a song to her. She was learning to be more vulnerable. I guess it was time to show that I was learning to be a kick-ass combat ninja.

Taste the Pain

"Uh," I said into the mic. "I was going to play some other song, but I'm not going to play that one now. This one's for my girl, who's standing in the back. It's called 'No Pain.'"

It started off quiet, but really fast and tense, lots of muted chords.

Every time I think that I have lost myself,
It's always just a case of being someone else.
And every time I think that there is someone dead,
I know that it's all just the games in my head.

No pain?
No pain.

Make believe myself in a thirty-second drop.
I don't believe in fortune or my luck to stop.
Fantasized fictional tragedy to feel.
When all is said and done, they seem like no big deal.

No pain?
No pain.

Here at the bridge was where I opened it up to some big, loud, fat chords and really sang out.

Sometimes I get a little confused.

And sometimes I feel a little abused.

It's okay to want a little pain.

And it's okay to want to be insane.

But on a night like this, I could be in the stars.

On a night like this, I could be in your arms.

This is our chance for a little romance,

This is our time to feel a little fine,

Soon the pain is gonna come back, see?

But until then, it's just you and me.

It went back to the original chords, but they were looser, messier now, with lots of little fills and riffs. Like it couldn't all be contained anymore.

Check my axle limping from a broken wheel.

Stick my fingers in my brain to cop a feel.

Radio heaven to nurse my darkest thoughts.

I cannot see beyond what I haven't got.

No pain?

No pain?

No pain?

No . . .

Taste the Pain

The last chord rang out in the room. I realized that I'd just done it. I sung in front of about fifty of my most judgmental peers.

Not only that, I'd also enjoyed it.

Afterward, Jen5 and I just kind of sprawled out together on an old stuffed couch. We'd both been so tense and worried, and now it was all over and we could finally relax. Raef came over with a mug of coffee.

"Killer song, bro," he said. "Here's my specialty. An Irish coffee." Then he winked at me, handed me the mug, and went back to the counter.

"Do you know what's in that?" asked Jen5 as I took a sip.

I coughed and nearly spit it back out into the cup.

"Irish whiskey, I'm guessing?" I said.

So we shared the mug of Irish coffee and basked in the compliments of friends and acquaintances.

Kick-ass combat ninja, rock-star style.

Addicted to Fame

13

It was Sunday and the usual rules applied. Mom wasn't putting on makeup or doing her hair, and she wasn't leaving the house. The problem was, she had a strong craving for a caramel macchiato. So of course I had to get it for her.

She handed me a twenty, said, "Get yourself something too," and then settled in to watch the entire third season of *Sex and the City* on DVD.

"Thanks," I said. "You know, kids aren't supposed to have caffeine. It stunts our growth."

"I'm trying to keep it from becoming taboo and therefore desirable," she said, and hit Play on the remote. "Is it working?"

"I think they have those organic juices," I said.

• • •

Addicted to Fame

There was a decent little coffee shop down the street and it was a nice day, so I just put my headphones on and walked. Sometimes there's nothing better to clear your head and get refocused. My mind wandered, but not in the crazy, hectic way it did at night. Instead it just floated along as the Clash's "Overpowered by Funk" was blasting from my MP3 player, conjuring up that feeling like I was in the opening credits of a movie. It was a biopic about the rise of indie rock legend Sammy Bojar. Did he know, at the age of seventeen, that one day he would be adored by millions, acclaimed by critics, and give new life to a genre that was beginning to slip into overmarketed mediocrity? How could he have had such depth and vision at that young age? And I was thinking Johnny Depp was way too old to play me, so maybe that Cillian Murphy guy, and Scarlett Johansson would play Jen5, of course. Who would play Rick? Jack Black, maybe? That cracked me up and I actually laughed a little out loud as I walked. But then I realized that by the time this movie was made, those actors would be way too old to play high school kids, even by Hollywood standards. But that was better, really. It would be young, unknown actors, getting their big breaks. And the kid who played me would study my concert videos and interviews to get my mannerisms and stuff, and he would look a lot like me, but with better hair and a cooler wardrobe. They'd have to keep the Boat the same, though. It was just too perfect—

Then my movie froze with one of those classic record-scratch sounds when I stepped through the front door of the coffee shop and saw Eric Strom, the lead singer of Monster Zero, standing behind the counter, serving coffee. I stopped in the doorway and just stared at him like a total idiot. In my head, the movie film had snapped and was flapping uselessly on the reel.

It didn't make any sense. This was the guy who was leading Columbus's claim to be "The Next Seattle." How could he possibly be making lattes in German Village? It would be like coming out of your house in the morning to go to school and finding out that Superman was your garbage collector.

He had just finished ringing up a customer and I guess he must have noticed me standing in the doorway staring at him because he looked right at me and smiled.

"Hey," he said, then pulled out a dirty, coffee-stained rag and began wiping the countertop.

"You . . . ," I said. "You're Eric Strom."

He looked at me kind of weird. "Do I know you?"

"Uh," I said. "Uh, no. I just . . . I'm a . . . I really like Monster Zero. I see all your shows."

"Awesome," he said. "Glad you like it." He smiled again and went back to wiping up the counter.

I thought about turning around, walking back home, getting in my car, and going to a completely different coffee shop. That's how freaked out I was. But that would have been just goofy. Even I knew that. So I walked to the counter and said, "I didn't know you worked here. I live right down the street and I'm pretty much here every Sunday and I never see you."

"Yeah," he said. "I usually work nights. But I switched shifts with someone so I could play a gig last week."

"At Saul's," I said.

"Yeah," he said. "Great venue."

"Yeah," I said. "You were great."

"Thanks," he said. He was totally getting weirded out by me now, but I couldn't help myself.

"I don't understand," I said.

"What?" he said.

"Why are you working in a coffee shop?"

"Uh . . . I don't like office jobs. And I need a flexible schedule for gigs."

"But you were named best indie rock band in Columbus," I said.

"Um, yeah," he said. "Like that actually means anything."

"But . . ."

"Listen, man. That's how it works. You're hot one minute, they make all sorts of promises, and a week later they've totally forgotten about you. Especially when you aren't interested in jumping through hoops for the big record labels." He looked at me for a minute. "You play?" he asked.

I nodded.

"What?"

"Guitar, mostly," I said.

"Cool," he said. "So you think we should be rock stars now that we were mentioned in a magazine?"

"Uh . . . ," I said.

"I'm only telling you this because I wish someone had told me when I was your age. It would have saved me a lot of heartache," he said. "See, you don't do it to become rich and famous. If that's what you want, go do something else, because for every one band that makes enough money off their music to live—and we're not talking a lot of money, just enough to live—for every one of those bands, there's ninety-nine that have to work crappy day jobs just so they can pay their rent. This is something you do because you love music and you gotta get it out there. And so you do whatever it takes."

He looked at me expectantly, with this hard expression on

his face, a glint of that punk rock stage god coming through in his eyes.

I just stared back at him. I didn't know what to say. I didn't even know what to think.

After a moment his expression softened. "Look, I'm sorry, kid. I didn't mean to dump all that on you." He smiled, a little forced. "Hey, maybe you should just think about doing something else. Like, I dunno, computers or something."

"There's nothing else," I said, quietly.

"Is that so?" he asked, his forced smile fading away. "Well, then. I hope you've got what it takes to stick it out. Wannabe rock stars are a dime a dozen, but real musicians? Those are actually pretty rare. Now, did you want some coffee?"

I ordered some coffee.

When I got home, Mom was doing that weird thing she always did when watching her *Sex and the City* where she laughs and cries at the same time.

"Here," I said, holding out her caramel macchiato.

"Thanks, sweetie," she said, her eyes still glued to whatever Sarah Jessica Parker was doing. It was an okay show, I guess. At least they actually showed the sex, instead of cutting the scene right before it got good. Although it had been the cause of many sex conversations between me and my mom, which mostly consisted of her telling me how rare it was to find a show with that much sexual honesty.

"Hey, Mom," I said. "What if I worked in a coffee shop my whole life?"

Mom grabbed the remote, switched off the TV, and turned to me with a look that probably froze both our coffee drinks.

"You're going to college," she said. "End of story."

"Huh?" I said.

"That's where this is going, isn't it?" she said.

"What? No. I just . . . well, what if I couldn't make enough money to completely support myself as a musician, and so I had to get another kind of job?"

"Well, since you're going to college, you won't have to worry about that, will you? You'll major in something useful and get a *real* job. A career job."

"But that's not what I want to do with my life. You always said that I should—"

"You could still play music. It would be your hobby."

"A *hobby*? That's like the worst word in the world. When you say that someone plays music as a hobby, you're saying they suck. Worse than that, you're saying they don't even *care* that they suck, 'cause it's just a hobby."

"You sound like your grandfather when you say that," she said, and clearly she didn't mean it as a compliment.

"Because I *am* like him. And that's all I want. To have a life like his. No stupid math or science or any of that. Just music."

"Sam, I know it all sounds so exciting and wonderful, but a real musician's life is difficult."

"I know that," I said.

"No, Sam. You don't. I do. Because I grew up with them. The late hours they kept. Always moving around from city to city. Never sure where the money would come from or when. The parties and drugs and booze. I didn't have any friends of my own because we never lived in one place long enough for me to make them. You think that was easy to grow up with? And do you think they were any happier because they were musicians? How do you think your grandmother Vivian died?"

"Uh . . . ," I said. "Heart attack, wasn't it?"

"Sure, that's the official story. But the heart attack was caused by a drug overdose. And there are generally two ways that overdoses happen. One is on purpose, the other is by accident. So your grandmother was either a suicide or a junkie or both. Sound like a great way to go? Jim Morrison, Kurt Cobain, and your grandmother. Hi-diddle-dee-dee, a musician's life for me, huh?"

What was it with people dumping on me today? She stared at me like I was supposed to respond to something like that. Like I even knew how the conversation got to that point. Yeah, maybe I'd been picking a little bit of a fight with her from the beginning. But it was like asking to arm wrestle with someone and instead they drop a nuke on your head.

"I'm going to go up to my room," I said. "To hide from the world."

Mom had already turned her DVD back on.

Later that day, I was on the phone with Jen5.

"Remember when you were telling me that your mom said she'd love you even if you worked at 7-Eleven?" I asked. "Well, *my* mom told me that she wouldn't."

"Oh, come on. Don't try to pretend like your mom is meaner than my mom. Your mom is actually pretty cool."

"Well, she's quickly becoming not cool."

"She's probably just worried that you have all this talent but you won't use it."

"No, what she's worried about is that I'll use the wrong kind of talent. She basically said she doesn't want me to be a musician because she's afraid I'd end up like my suicidal junkie grandmother."

"Your grandmother was a suicidal junkie?"

"That's what my mom claims. She said, and I quote, 'Jim Morrison, Kurt Cobain, and your grandmother.'"

"Wow," said Jen5. "That's actually kind of cool."

"You're not helping."

"What do you want me to do? Talk to your mom for you? Explain why it is that you want to be a rock star?"

"Well, that's the other thing. I went to the coffee shop by my house today, and get this: Eric Strom from Monster Zero was working there."

"So?"

"Besides the fact that the singer for one of the best bands in the Midwest has to have a day job? He basically said that most musicians need to have other jobs just to pay the rent."

"So do artists. So does pretty much everyone with a cool job in this lame-ass country."

"I guess I hadn't really thought about it before. I mean . . . that everything I want could come true, I could be as good as Eric Strom, and I'd *still* have to work some shitty job. It just doesn't seem right, you know?"

"In the Czech Republic, the government actually gives money to artists so they can concentrate on art instead of how they're going to pay the rent," said Jen5. "That's why everything we put out in America these days is such crap. Because it's survival of the most commercial here."

"None of that helps me," I said.

"Well, you could move to Prague."

"Thanks."

"What? I'd move with you. I think I'd really like living in Europe."

"Maybe someday. But for right now, what do I do?"

"I don't know. Tell her you want to major in music composition so that you can write motion picture soundtracks or something. That sounds nice and boring with very little risk of suicide or hard drugs."

"Become a soulless marketing minion?"

"Hey, now. My uncle works in PR and he is without a doubt the coolest person in my family."

"But still, it just seems so . . ."

"Sam, you're missing the point. You don't actually have to write commercial jingles or action movie soundtracks. You just major in it and get the knowledge from studying music, and you tell her that's what you'll do with the knowledge. But in reality, you'll do whatever you want, and by then you'll have graduated from college and so it won't matter."

"Oh," I said. "You know, that might actually work."

"And then," she said, "you can meet me in Prague."

The phone beeped.

"Hang on," I said. "There's someone on the other line." I clicked over and said, "Hello?"

"Hey," said a low, gravelly voice.

"Joe?"

"Yeah. I really need to talk to you. Can you meet me? I'm at the Dube."

"Um . . . ," I said. "Sure."

"Great," he said, not sounding especially enthusiastic. "See you soon." Then he hung up.

I clicked back over to Jen5.

"That was weird," I said. "It was Joe. He wants to meet up with me."

"Oh, God, Sammy, you didn't say yes, did you?"

"Of course I did," I said. "Why wouldn't I?"

"Well, I thought after what happened . . ."

"Fiver, I'm not scared of him anymore. I think we might actually be able to be friends now."

"Why would you want to be?"

"Somebody should be," I said.

The Blue Danube, or as most people called it, the Dube, was a bar and restaurant just off the OSU campus. It was a pretty seedy place, and the food was lousy. It was just one big open room, with the bar on one side, and a bunch of booths and tables on the other. It was kind of like a diner with a good jukebox and mood lighting. In fact, there were hardly any regular lights in the Dube. Just one or two small lamps over by the bar. Most of the lighting for the place came from a big blue neon sign hung above the booths that said THE BLUE DUBE in swirling script. The sign cast everything in a dim blue light, making the place feel like it was a scene from some gritty crime movie.

Joe was sitting over in the corner booth, directly beneath the Blue Dube sign. He was writing in a little blank book, an empty coffee cup in front of him and a cigarette burning in the ashtray. Even directly under the sign, I couldn't imagine how he was able to see what he was writing without serious eyestrain. One hand was wrapped in a thick bandage.

"Hey," I said, sliding into the booth.

He didn't respond right away, but instead continued to scribble into his book. I knew that feeling. Just wanted to finish that one last thought before it was gone. So I sat and listened to the jukebox. It was playing "Just Like Honey," an old Jesus and Mary Chain song—slow, fat, distorted guitar under whispered vocals. It really was a great jukebox.

Joe put down his pen and snapped his little blank book closed.

"Hey," he said.

"What's up?" I asked.

"Sorry about what happened," he said, his eyes trailing to his bandaged hand.

"That's okay," I said. "I wasn't the one who got hurt."

"I heard you played at an open mic at Idiot Child last night."

"Yeah," I said. "I just did one song. It was mainly for Jen5's art show."

He nodded and started clicking his Zippo lighter open and closed with his good hand. The sharp *ping* sound it made was in counterpoint to the song in the background. There was a faint smell of lighter fluid that penetrated the greasy burger smell.

"I need this band," he said suddenly. He was looking directly at me, with the same expression as when I gave him a ride home. That sad, broken look. "I know I've said a lot of shit about it, and about you guys. But that was just me talking. I know I'm not a great musician like you and TJ. I know that." Then his face went from that broken look to the triumphant, confident look that he had when we first saw that poster about the Battle of the Bands. "This band is special," he said in a way that you couldn't argue with. "It's going to *be* something. I know it. We can still kick ass at this contest. And you know I'll work my ass off, because it's the only worthwhile thing I have now," he said.

"Yeah," I said. "I know that feeling."

"So, are we keeping the band together?" he asked.

The question totally floored me. Because I hadn't realized it was my decision. And now, before I said anything, I had to decide for myself. I'd had a lot of dreams about this band becoming something. Was I going to give up on those dreams now, less than a week away from a contest that might make us that one percent that didn't have to have day jobs? Or was I going to see this through?

"You have to be cool with TJ and Laurie dating," I said.

"Yeah," he said. "I can handle it."

"And nobody likes getting yelled at in rehearsal."

He sighed. "I get it. I was a dick. I'm sorry. I'll be cool from now on."

"And," I said, "if we're still going to do this Battle of the Bands thing on Thursday, you have to have the lyrics to the songs we're doing memorized."

"That's like three days away," he said. "No problem."

"Let's do it, then. I'll call Rick and TJ and we can rehearse tomorrow after school."

"Awesome," said Joe, actually showing a real smile. Then he said, "Uh, we should probably do your songs for the contest. Mine's not really ready for prime time yet."

"Yeah," I said. "Good idea."

Everything in Its Right Place

14

"You did what?" asked Jen5 the next day at lunch. Everyone else at the table—Rick, TJ, Alexander, and Laurie—were all giving me the same shocked look, but Jen5 was the only one to speak up.

"I told him it was cool," I said. "Come on, guys. Give him a chance."

"Sammy, what about *your* chance? I thought you were going to do your own thing now."

"I'd never be able to get anything together in time for the contest."

"Why do you even care about the contest?" she asked.

"I don't know . . ."

"Didn't you say that you thought music competitions were lame?"

"Yeah, they are. But think about getting that studio time. We can't pass that up. Maybe if we got a killer song on the radio, I wouldn't have to work at a coffee shop or write commercials."

"Sammy," she said.

"Come on, Fiver," I said. "I want this so bad. Just back me up on this one, okay?"

She looked at me for a moment, then sighed. "Of course I will, Sammy."

I could tell the whole thing bothered Jen5, but I couldn't figure out why. Working things out with the band had seemed to make much more sense than starting all over again. Maybe she just thought I should be the frontman or something. But when it came down to it, I didn't need to be the guy that everyone looked at. It was nice to fantasize about, but in reality, it wasn't that important to me. I just cared about the music.

I was pretty nervous before rehearsal. As much as I hoped things would go well, I was about fifty percent sure that it would all fall apart at rehearsal. Something would set Joe off and he'd just go ballistic on all of us. Or if nothing else, having gone so long without rehearsal, nobody would remember what we were doing.

But amazingly enough, we actually sounded good. It helped that we just drilled the same three songs over and over again. And Rick did get a little confused every once in a while. But as soon as he got lost, he knew it immediately and fixed it himself. There were also a few times when Joe forgot his lyrics, but he'd immediately grab the sheet and look at it and get back on track. One time, he even apologized.

We took breaks in between songs and popped open the emergency exit door. We hung out on the back steps by the loading dock. Joe and Rick passed cigarettes back and forth while we all talked about little things we could add to the songs to make them even better, or how we were going to kick ass at the contest. Then we started talking about what we were going to do when we won. Should we send the track we recorded to a bunch of music blogs? Should we have a little tour? Rick had a cousin in Cincinnati who might be able to get in touch with a place down there, and Joe knew a bunch of people in Cleveland. It felt good to talk like that. It felt like we were a real band. We even sounded like a real band.

And maybe, for the first time, we were.

• • •

I gave Rick a ride home as usual.

"I have to swing by Marigold's to pick up some new strings," I said as we climbed into the car.

"Okay," he said. I could tell something was on his mind. He was working himself up to something serious. You couldn't rush Rick on stuff like that, so I just waited.

We had been driving for about ten minutes in silence when Rick suddenly blurted out, "You should do your own thing. Drop Joe and do your own thing."

"But it's all coming together," I said. "We sounded great tonight."

"Tonight," said Rick. "Who knows what he'll be like tomorrow."

"Maybe he's really changed," I said. "Maybe it took all that to make him understand."

"Maybe," said Rick.

"You think he's faking it?" I asked.

"I don't think he's faking it."

"What, then?"

"I'm sure he thinks he's turned over a new leaf. But changing isn't as easy as that. People try to be better all the time. Who doesn't want to be better? But most of the time, people screw it up."

"Wow," I said. "Have you considered joining the pep

squad? What about winning the contest and going on a tour? What about everything we talked about tonight?"

"That's all it was, Sammy," said Rick. "Just talk."

"I don't believe that," I said.

"I know you don't," he said, and he sounded kind of sad.

Marigold's was mainly a CD store, but they had a little guitar supply section in the back that sold my brand of strings. It was a little cheaper than the guitar shop and a lot closer to home. I was tempted to stop at the New Release section to see what was out, but I really didn't have the money to buy new music, so we just made a beeline for the strings. We were back at the front, waiting in line for the register, in a only few minutes.

"I might actually get out of here without buying something I don't need," I said to Rick.

"That would be a first," he said.

I noticed he was standing very close to me and his eyes kept flickering over my shoulder at something behind me. Like he was hiding from something.

"What is it?" I said, turning my head.

"Don't turn around," he whispered quietly.

"Rick?" came a cheerful voice behind me.

"Too late," Rick growled under his breath. Then he smiled and said, "Hey, Zeke."

I turned and saw a guy with long blond hair pulled back in a ponytail. He was wearing a tight black T-shirt and jeans that most guys I know would be way too self-conscious to pull off. Maybe it was the jeans that made me think he was gay. Or maybe it was the fact that when he looked at Rick, it was completely obvious he had a crush on him.

"How are you?" Zeke asked him with a sincerity that was kind of intense.

"Uh, okay, I guess," said Rick, looking very uncomfortable. "This is . . ."—he gestured at me.

"Oh, hey, I saw you play at the open mic on Saturday," said Zeke. "Jen5's friend, right? Sammy? You were awesome!"

"Thanks," I said. "You know Jen5?"

"Yeah, we used to go to art summer school at the College of Art and Design."

"Cool," I said. "So you're a painter too?"

"I'm nowhere near as good as Jen5," said Zeke.

"She's awesome," I agreed.

"Music's more my thing," he said.

"No kidding," I said. "What do you play?"

"Keyboard, mainly. More like electronic stuff." He held up the CD he had just bought. "The new VFSix."

"I've never heard of them," I admitted. "I honestly don't follow the electronica scene much."

"They have sort of a trip-hop, downbeat sound," said Zeke.

"Oh, like Portishead?"

"Yeah, kinda." He nodded. "But a lot jazzier, almost like Booker T."

"That sounds awesome," I said.

"They're based out of Moscow," he said. "There's a huge downbeat scene coming out of there right now."

"I totally have to check into that," I said. "I mean, it's not really my thing, but you never know. Maybe we could—"

"Okay!" said Rick, a little too loud. "Sammy, the guy at the register is waiting. Don't hold up the line."

There was one guy in line behind us, reading a magazine, not looking like he was in any kind of hurry.

"Sure . . . ," I said. "Well, nice meeting you, Zeke."

"You too," said Zeke. "Tell Jen5 I said hi." Then he looked at Rick and there was something kind of wistful in his voice when he said, "See you later, Rick."

"Right, cool," said Rick, practically shoving me at the register.

Once we were safely back in the car, I turned to Rick. "We totally have to start hanging out with that guy," I said. "I can't remember the last time I could geek out about music with someone so quickly."

"*You* can hang out with him," said Rick. He was slouched extra-low in his seat, his arms crossed.

"What is up with you?" I asked. "Is it because he likes you?"

"What? You're crazy," he said, not sounding at all convincing.

"Dude, he's totally into you. I don't know much about gay dating, but my friggin' grandfather could see it."

"Yeah, okay, Francine and Fiver were trying to hook me up with him on Saturday."

"Of course they were," I said. "Because he's awesome!"

"Will you just . . . start the car, okay?"

"Are you blushing?" I asked.

"Please. Start. The goddamn. Car."

We drove for a little while in silence.

"Seriously," I said. "Is he not good-looking or something?"

"Can we please not talk about this?"

"Come on, Rick. I'm not teasing anymore," I said. "I'm just trying to understand."

Rick stared out of the window for a full minute before he said, "Yes, he is good-looking."

"I only talked to him for a minute, but he seems like a nice guy."

"He's very nice," agreed Rick.

"He's a painter and a musician. That's cool."

"He's very cool," said Rick.

"Do you think he's . . . hot?" It felt kind of weird to say it, but that was just because I wasn't used to referring to guys as "hot."

"Jesus, Sammy!" Rick threw his hands into the air. "Yes, I think he's hot, okay? Are we done now?"

"Then why were you such a total dick to him tonight?" I asked.

"Because I'm just not interested in doing anything with anyone right now."

"Okay, sure," I said. "That's fine. I just—"

"I know," said Rick. "Thanks for your concern. I'm cool."

We drove the rest of the way without saying another word. Finally, when I stopped in front of his house and he started to climb out, I said, "Rick."

He stopped, one leg still in the car.

"I just . . . It doesn't seem fair. To you. I dump all my crap on you all the time, but you keep yours all bottled up. You should be able to dump stuff back on me."

He looked at me for a moment, and I thought I'd seen every expression he had. But I didn't recognize this one at all.

"I know, Sammy," he said quietly. "I'm sorry. I just . . . can't. Not yet. Okay?"

"Okay," I said.

"Good night, Sammy."

"Good night, Rick."

I got home later than usual, so I expected Mom to be home already. But she wasn't. In fact, I was halfway through my homework by the time I heard her come through the door. And I was finished with it by the time she'd made her way from the wine bottle to my room.

"Hey, Sammy," she said. She looked tired, and her makeup was a little smudged. The only time that ever happened was when she'd been crying.

"Everything okay, Mom?" I asked. I was at my usual place, sitting cross-legged on the floor with my guitar on my lap.

"I've just been over at your grandfather's house most of the night."

"How is he?" I asked.

"Well . . ." She sat down heavily on my bed. "He refused to come out of the bathroom the entire time I was there. He kept muttering something about a secret code hidden in album covers."

Everything in Its Right Place

"What?"

She shrugged. "I have no idea. And I took a look in the freezer and my guess is that he hasn't eaten anything since you were there."

I shook my head. "He didn't eat when I was there. He just threw it away."

"So it's been even longer, then," she said. Then she sighed and massaged her temples with her fingertips. "I think that's it, then. We can't put it off any longer. I'll go down and talk to someone at the assisted-living facility tomorrow."

"A nursing home," I said. "He's not going to like it."

"Sammy, we can't take care of him anymore. He's like a child, really. He needs professional, around-the-clock care. I'm concerned that if we don't do something soon, he could hurt himself."

Part of me agreed with her, of course. I knew that Gramps shouldn't be on his own anymore. And maybe Jen5 was right and he'd be much happier hanging with other crazy old people. But I felt like I understood him better than anybody else. And I wondered if he really would want that life. I knew I didn't. In fact, I think I probably would have chosen to die living my own life than live in some kind of institution.

Of course, that was easy for me to say, because it wasn't

happening to me. What would he say if he were still the real Gramps?

Mom got up off my bed and sat down next to me on the floor.

"I'm sorry, sweetie. But it's for the best."

I nodded. Speaking seemed a little too hard right then, since my throat felt like it was filled with a lead weight.

"So, while I'm looking at places tomorrow, I need to you check in on him after school. Maybe you can get him to eat. Or at least come out of the bathroom."

"We were going to have practice tomorrow," I said. "The contest is only in three days."

"Sammy, your grandfather needs you," she said.

"I know," I said.

"You'll still have Wednesday night to rehearse."

"Yeah," I said. "That's better than nothing."

I knew she was really worried about Gramps, because she didn't even think to hassle me about still being in a band with Joe.

Sins of the Father

15

I drove over to Gramps's place the next day. He didn't answer the door when I knocked. That was usual. But then I tried to open the door and it was locked. Weird. He never locked his front door. Mom and I had been trying to get him to do it for years and he'd refused. But now, suddenly, he locked it?

I knocked again, louder, and still nothing. I started to get worried. That he'd accidentally hurt himself. That he'd purposely hurt himself. That he'd had a heart attack or an aneurysm or one of those other old-people things that came up suddenly. I banged on the door one last time. Should I call Mom? The cops? The medics? Just as I was about to turn around and go back to the Boat, I heard the deadbolt slide. The door opened a crack and Gramps peered out. The look in his eyes was something I'd never seen before. It was pure, 100 percent insanity.

"Thank God you're here," he said, then grabbed my arm. His grip was surprisingly strong. He jerked me inside and slammed the door shut and locked it. The place was weirdly silent. Not even one album playing. Scraps of paper and broken records were scattered everywhere. The whole place stank like old garbage and new piss.

"I was worried she'd gotten you," he mumbled. He was wearing a yellow rubber raincoat and boots and nothing else, and there was something really creepy about that. "I knew she'd already gotten Viv, damn her. But at least she didn't get you. You made it. Just barely, but you did."

"Gramps, what's going on?" I asked. "Who were you worried had gotten me?"

"Oh, you know," he frowned and gestured vaguely. "Her. The one who keeps me here."

"Have you eaten anything today, Gramps?"

"Ha! Are you kidding? Everything's poisoned!"

"Gramps, it's not poisoned. Look, how about I make you something?"

He shook his head vehemently. "For all I know, she's already gotten to you."

"Gramps, what are you talking about?"

"Listen," he said, leaning in like some kind of cartoon spy. "It's time you know the truth about me. I'm not really a socialist sympathizer."

"No?"

"No, I'm a double agent planted by the CIA to draw out potential threats and mark them for nullification."

The strangest part was that he was so sure of himself, for a split second I actually believed him. In fact, my first thought was, *Oh my God, is he about to arrest me?* But then I realized that he had fully gone off the deep end. His eyes were wide and they rolled around in their wrinkled sockets. His mouth was pulled back in something that was probably supposed to look like a smile, but it made him look more like a grinning skull. Then I saw something flash in his hand. It was the end of a pair of scissors. He was hiding the rest up his sleeve. When I saw that, it suddenly didn't matter if he was my grandfather or not. He was just a scary crazy old guy with a concealed sharp object.

"So . . . ," I struggled. "You don't need any food?"

"No, no, no! Don't you see? It's all poisoned!"

"And there's nothing else you need?"

"What do you think I am?" It came out like a snarl. "*Helpless?*"

I didn't even recognize him anymore. His face was twisted up into a sneer and he moved restlessly around the living room, knocking things over and tripping on piles of paper and books.

I backed slowly toward the door.

"What are you doing?" he demanded. "You can't leave! She's out there!"

"I have to go, Gramps." My voice was high and shaking. "Sorry . . ." I didn't know what to say, couldn't tell if he even understood, and didn't care. I just ran.

I drove home as fast as the Boat would let me. I practically ran inside the house. Mom was sitting at the dinner table, going through big stacks of paper.

"Mom, something is really wrong with Gramps."

She looked up immediately. "Did you call 911?"

"No." My hands hadn't stopped shaking the whole drive home. The adrenaline just wouldn't leave me. "He's not . . . he's not sick or anything like that. He just . . . he's really lost it."

"Calm down, Sammy," she said. "Tell me what happened."

So as best I could, I told her everything. It seemed to help a little. By the end, my hands weren't shaking anymore and I was breathing regularly. The whole time, Mom listened quietly. The only time she interrupted me was when I told her about the scissors he had hidden up his sleeve.

"You're sure?" she asked. "It couldn't have been something else? Like his watch?"

"I—I don't think so . . ." It had been dark. He had been so wild, so crazy. All I'd been able to concentrate on was getting out of there.

"Okay, Sammy," said Mom, she walked over to me and put her hands firmly on my shoulders. "You did fine. Just slow down a little. I'm finishing up the paperwork for the assisted living right now. They told me that as luck would have it, they have a space opening up this weekend."

"This weekend? But what are we going to do *now*?"

"I'll check on him tomorrow morning before my first client."

"That's all you're going to do? You're just going to let him be a raving lunatic all night?"

"Sam, did it seem like there was any way you could calm him down?"

"Well, no . . ."

"If he's physically endangering himself or someone else, we can call the police. Is that want you want to do?"

"Of course not! But he's like some kind of . . . animal. It's awful. Just thinking of him being like that all night . . ."

"I understand that you're upset, Sammy," she said. "I'm sorry. There's nothing else we can do."

I lay in bed for what seemed like forever, unable to get the picture out of my head of Gramps looking like some kind of psycho killer. I tried to find that calm control I'd had when I'd taken Joe to the hospital. Right then, I didn't care if it made me into Robot Boy or whatever. If I could get into that headspace again, I knew I'd be able to go right to sleep. And that was all I wanted. Just to stop thinking.

But I couldn't. My brain was like a washing machine, sloshing with all of Gramps's genetic craziness that had somehow skipped Mom and landed right on me.

After a while, I couldn't take it anymore. I got out of bed, grabbed my guitar, and started playing. I didn't care how late it was or how loud I got, and I guess Mom didn't either because she didn't bang on her wall like she usually did. I played until my hand hurt. Until my fingertips were red and raw despite the calluses I'd built up. Then I grabbed my notebook and in a wild spurt wrote the final verse to "Plastic Baby" and it all came together:

Cain is dead forever.
Make believe forever.

Sins of the Father

Reason doesn't matter.
Tell you what I'm after,

Clothes and smiles of rubber
Whore instead of lover
Talk with no conversation
Live with no realization

Make-believe is luring.
Fantasy's obscuring.
It's like feeling through plastic gloves.
It's like feeling through plastic gloves.

And that's when I understood that I had the title of the song wrong. I hooked in a comma and now it said: *Plastic, Baby.*

It wasn't a judgment.

It was a wish. Because sometimes I was tired of feeling so *much* and I just wanted to shut down and not feel anything. But I guess I wasn't wired that way. All I could do was write about it. Get it out of my head and onto something like paper that I could manage easier. When Gramps and Eric Strom had talked about music being something you just had to get out there, that is what they meant.

And it worked. When I was done playing, my hands

throbbed, my throat was sore, and the neighbors probably hated me. But I didn't care. Because I lay back in bed with that song still looping in my head, and I went right to sleep.

The next morning I felt a little better. While I was eating breakfast, Mom said that I shouldn't worry. That she was going over to Gramps's house right away and that she'd do whatever needed to be done.

"Don't even think about it," she said. "After all, don't you have that contest tomorrow night? You need to rehearse with your band."

I didn't know why Mom was suddenly down with me doing the Battle of the Bands. Maybe she felt bad that I was so tweaked the night before. But I wasn't going to argue. And if the current good fellowship held, Tragedy of Wisdom could actually win this thing. I would talk to them all at lunch and get them hyped for rehearsal.

That was the plan, at least.

I was in Ms. Jansen's English class, my head propped up in my hands as I tried to at least look like I was paying attention. My mind kept wandering off into daydreams. The concert, and our song on the radio, and record labels begging us to lay down an album and us telling them to get lost. Laughing in their uptight corporate faces. Or maybe they would love us so much they wouldn't ask us to change anything, wanted us just the way we were. So we said okay, okay, we'll cut your stupid album, but no cheesy videos. And all the while my mom telling me to still try to not flunk any of my classes, and groupies screaming for us every weekend at the local venues . . .

To-morrow, and to-morrow, and to-morrow,
Creeps in this petty pace from day to day,
To the last syllable of recorded time;
And all our yesterdays have lighted fools
The way to dusty death. Out, out, brief candle!

Ms. Jansen had this way of busting into a dramatic reading from whatever thing we were studying at random times to wake us up. It worked pretty well because she had such a loud, ringing voice, and since she was the director of the school plays, she was actually kind of a good actor.

Now that she was sure she had our attention, she gazed around the room and said, "That is from Act Five of *Macbeth*, which I know you read last night, yes? Can someone tell me what they think he's saying in this monologue?"

Silence.

"Samuel? How about you?"

"Uh," I said. "Sure. Okay. So uh, here's Macbeth, right? Watching this army coming to get him. He knows that he's done really bad stuff. He knows his wife is dead, I think. Or at least he's pretty sure. I can't remember exactly. And he knows now that all the prophecies the witches gave him were tricks, that they're all coming true even though they seemed impossible, and he's going to be beheaded and stuff really soon. He knows all that. What he doesn't know is if it matters."

"If what matters?" asked Ms. Jansen.

"Everything," I said. "Did he have any choices ever? Could he have said, 'No, I don't want to kill the king' and escaped all of it? It seems like no matter what he wanted to do, it wouldn't have made a difference. It was fate. So he's kind of like, 'Yesterday, today, tomorrow, what's the difference?' because he doesn't feel like he ever had a choice."

"Very interesting, Samuel. And I think in a lot of ways you're right. What Macbeth has gained is clarity. He's gotten perspective on how the whole thing fits together, and he doesn't see a pretty picture. Take this next section, which I think speaks for itself:

> *Life's but a walking shadow, a poor player,*
> *That struts and frets his hour upon the stage,*

Sins of the Father

And then is heard no more. It is a tale
Told by an idiot, full of sound and fury,
Signifying nothing.

Ms. Jansen looked around at us, that drama flair kicking in, letting the words sink into our heads.

"Have any of *you* ever felt like that?" she asked. "Like you've been miscast in your role in life? Like you're a . . . what do you guys call it . . . a wannabe?"

"But isn't that a cop-out?" I asked. "Isn't he, like, playing the victim or whatever? Making excuses?"

"*He* doesn't seem to think so," said Ms. Jansen. "He sees absolutely no hope." But she's looking at me like she's expecting me to argue.

"So?" I asked. "Which is it? Did he have a choice or not?"

"Maybe sometimes things happen that *are* out of your control," she said. "But you *always* have a choice in how you deal with it."

Then the intercom crackled: "Would Samuel Bojar please come to the principal's office immediately."

Ms. Jansen looked at me questioningly. I shrugged like I had no idea. Because I didn't. In fact, my pulse was suddenly pounding in my temples. There's nothing worse than being in trouble for something and you don't know what it is.

"You'd better go," she said.

I stood up, trying not to look as nervous and confused as I felt. I caught Joe out of the corner of my eye, looking at me with a sly grin. I smiled back and shrugged like, *Hey, what can you do?* The other students snickered and giggled as I left the classroom.

When I got to the principal's office, his secretary gave me a weird look. Almost like sympathy. I'd never been called to the principal's office before, so I thought maybe this was normal. Like maybe she had a soft spot for troublemakers. Not that I could think of anything I'd done wrong.

"Go on in, Samuel," she said.

I stepped into the room. Principal Scott was sitting behind his desk. He was a big black guy with a furrowed brow like he had the weight of the world on his shoulders. Or at least the weight of the high school, which was probably true. Standing next to his desk was our spacey guidance counselor, Mr. Liven. Neither of them looked angry, but they both looked very serious. That kind of threw me. Mr. Scott never smiled, but Mr. Liven was one of those eternally cheerful guys who liked to greet every student he walked past in the hallway by name. I stopped and waited in the doorway, not sure what to do next.

"Samuel, have a seat," said Mr. Scott.

Sins of the Father

I sat down in the chair facing his desk. It was a little low, so I had to look up at them.

"Samuel," said Mr. Scott. "There's been a . . ." He seemed unsure what word to use. Finally, he said, "An accident. Your mother is in the hospital. She's going to be fine. But it's probably best if you go and see her right away."

At first I didn't understand. There was some kind of delay as the words worked their way into my brain. Mom? Hurt? Then suddenly it was really hard to breathe, to get air into my lungs. I had to fight to say, "What . . . what happened?"

Mr. Scott and Mr. Liven exchanged glances. Then Mr. Scott said, "We don't really know all the details. We just know she's stable and has been transferred to a regular room from the ER." He shuffled some papers on his desk so he didn't have to look at me. "Do you have any family nearby?"

"Just my grandfather," I said.

They looked at each other again. Then Mr. Scott said, "Would you like Mr. Liven to drive you to the hospital?"

"No thanks," I said. "I'll go by myself."

There weren't that many times when industrial metal really went with my life. But this was one of those moments. The guttural screams and crunching guitar of Ministry's "Burning Inside" hurled through the open car windows and out into the street as I drove down to the hospital. I didn't need to think or feel. The music did all that for me, far better than I ever could. I weaved in and out of traffic and made it to the hospital in record time. I walked inside, industrial thrash still humming in my veins as I gave my name to the lady at the info desk, and they told me where to go.

But when I walked into the room, the Ministry bravado left as quick as it had come. The first thing I saw was that the left side of mom's head had been shaved bald. Running in a curved line from the top of her head to her temple on that bald side was a row of staples. She was asleep, but I could tell her left eye was swollen shut. There were also a lot of bruises on her face, neck, and arms.

People had always told me my mother was beautiful. It was such a weird thing to hear and I never really understood it. She was just my mom. But now I finally saw it. I don't know why it took bruises, black eyes, staples, and a half-shaved head to show me. Why hadn't I appreciated it before now?

Then her eyes flickered and opened. She looked at me blankly for a second and I got a sudden sick fear that she didn't recognize me. But then her lips moved and she said hoarsely, "Sammy?"

"I'm here, Mom." I walked over and took her hand, careful not to mess up the IV.

Sins of the Father

"I'm sorry, Sammy," she said, her eyes unfocused. "I'm sorry you have to see this. I'm sorry it happened."

"What happened?" I asked.

"I went to Gramps's house and the door was locked, like you said. I rang the bell and knocked but there was no answer. I have a key, of course, so I just let myself in. I had a minute to look around. To see the mess. The trash, the puddle of urine in the corner. The rotten food on the table. Then I hear this crazy scream and I see Dad wearing nothing but a white bedsheet wrapped around himself like a toga. He has something in his hand and at first I can't make it out. Then as he gets closer and raises his hand over his head, I see that it's a big plumber's wrench. I should have done something, but I didn't. I just couldn't believe my own father could do something like that."

She closed her eyes and I thought maybe she'd passed out. But then, with her eyes still closed, she said, "Stupid. I know better. I know what people are capable of." She opened her good eye again but didn't look at me. Instead she stared at the ceiling. "He hits me with the wrench. He's screaming something at me. I don't know what. I somehow get back to the door and he's chasing me, hitting me again and again. On the head. On the back. On the arm. Wherever he can. I get outside and he's still after me. I guess neighbors saw what was happening. The cops show up at some point. He's not hitting me anymore, thank God. I'm lying on the lawn and he's just standing over me screaming and waving that wrench around." She closed her eyes again. "The last thing I saw before I blacked out was that he was so wild, it took three cops to restrain him."

Then her eyes slowly closed. I wasn't sure if she was going to say something, so I just waited. But after a few minutes, she started snoring a little bit.

A nurse came in and started checking her monitors.

"Are you Samuel?" she asked.

"Yeah," I said.

"You'll be able to take her home tonight, but we want to keep her under observation for a few more hours. You can stay with her, but you should try to let her sleep as much as possible."

"Okay," I said. "Where's my grandfather?"

She stopped fussing with the monitors. "He's been sedated."

"But where is he?"

"Well, he's in the psychiatric hospital right now. He'll be evaluated and then later moved to an assisted-living facility. The people there will make sure he stays on his medicine and that he doesn't hurt anyone else."

I nodded and the nurse left. I sat down next to Mom's bed and waited.

Sins of the Father

• • •

The next thing I remember, a nurse was gently shaking me awake.

"Your friends are here," she said.

"Friends?" I said stupidly. I turned to the doorway and there they were: Rick, TJ, Alexander, Joe, Laurie, and Jen5, all huddled together, almost like that would keep them safe.

The nurse told them to talk quietly and not to wake up Mom, then she left. They stared at me like they had no idea what to do now that they were here. They looked so bewildered that under any other circumstances, I probably would have laughed. But right now it seemed more sad than funny. It was like this room and this experience had separated me from them. Made me different. And even though both sides wanted to cross over, we didn't know how. And it was like that for a long time, with us just staring like it was an uncrossable chasm.

Then, Jen5 said, "Okay, okay, enough," then elbowed her way past the others, walked over to me, and hugged me hard. At first, my body tensed up. I didn't feel like touching anyone. But as she continued to squeeze me with her strong, thin arms, I started to trust that strength, and so I relaxed and even leaned into her a little. I slowly wrapped my arms around her. Then I put my face in her mass of frizzy blond hair and inhaled that familiar smell.

"Thank you for coming," I said.

She nodded into my chest. Her shoulders started shaking and I realized she was crying.

I looked at the rest of them and tried to smile, tried to show them I was okay. That it was all okay. They smiled back like they believed me and I really appreciated that, even if it wasn't true.

"Thanks, guys," I said. "I . . . uh . . . I know we were supposed to rehearse tonight, but . . . I, uh . . ."

"Don't even think about it," said TJ. "Seriously."

"I just . . . I don't want to let you guys down," I said.

"You need to take care of yourself right now," said Rick.

I nodded.

"So . . . do you need anything?" asked TJ.

"No, I'm cool," I said. That almost made me laugh after all. It seemed so dumb to say.

"Are you going home tonight?" asked Rick.

"We both are," I said. "They just want to keep her under observation right now."

They all nodded again. In unison. This time, I did laugh a little.

"You all go home," I said. "Thanks for coming." Then, because it sounded a little dismissive, I said, "Really. Thanks."

Sins of the Father

They all slowly filed out, except Jen5, who was still clinging to me, her face still pressed into my shoulder.

"Can I stay?" she asked, her voice muffled.

"Sure," I said. "I think that would be nice."

For the next few hours, my mom slept and I told Jen5 everything about Gramps. Not just the new stuff, but everything. Usually I told her the funny stuff, like his obsession with McCarthy, but I'd always leave out the scary parts. And when I told her about it all now, she listened. Really listened.

Then she told me about her own grandfather, who was dead now. He had been an orthopedic surgeon and a nut about golf. He didn't like kids, though, so most of her memories were of him sitting in his La-Z-Boy, wearing his plaid pants, watching golf on TV, and drinking straight bourbon all morning. He also never used denture cream, or maybe it got dissolved by all the bourbon, and whenever he laughed, which wasn't often, or yelled, which was a lot, his teeth would float around in his mouth.

After she finished telling me about her grandfather, she asked me about my dad.

I didn't really even like thinking about the dad thing. But I guess a lot of people wondered about it. I'd never talked about it to anyone before.

"I don't know," I said. "He was just some guy my mom was dating in college. When they found out she was pregnant, he freaked and split. We don't have any idea where he is, and I don't think my mom wants to know."

"Do you?"

I shrugged. "Sometimes. When I get that feeling like something's missing, you know? And I wonder if that's what it is. Like I'm a puzzle and there's a great big hole right where the dad piece goes. But when I was a kid, I didn't feel that way. When I had Gramps, like he used to be, I felt like I had something better than anyone else. Something better than a dad."

"Do you think you'll ever try to find him?"

"Maybe someday," I said. "But not anytime soon. I want to be my own man before I meet him. Just in case."

"In case what?"

"In case he's a total asshole."

A little while later, Mom woke up.

"Christ," she said, her voice soft and scratchy. "I feel like hell."

Then her eyes came into focus and she looked around. "Oh, hi, Jennifer," she said. "Thanks for keeping Sammy company. That's very sweet."

"I'm just glad you're okay, Ms. B," said Jen5.

"Yeah," said Mom. "So am I." She sat up carefully and looked around. "Okay, let's get a nurse in here and find out how soon they'll spring us from this joint."

Two hours later, we were in the Boat and heading home. But first we dropped Jen5 off at her house.

As she climbed out of the backseat, she said, "See you tomorrow in school?"

"I guess so," I said.

"Good-bye, Ms. B," she said. Then she started walking up the driveway toward her front door.

Mom rolled down her window and called out, "Wait a sec, Jennifer." Then she turned back to me and looked at me sternly. In the Mom Authority voice that she hardly ever used, she said, "Samuel Bojar, I thought I raised you better than that. You get out of this car and go give that girl a good-bye kiss."

I stared at her in disbelief.

"What?" she said. "You didn't think I knew you guys were dating?"

"Well . . . ," I said.

"Sammy. She's waiting."

I nodded, got out of the Boat, and walked over to where Jen5 was standing and looking a little confused.

"Thanks again for staying with me," I said. Then, before she could respond, I stepped in and kissed her. I meant for it to be one of those quick pecks. Who wants to make out in front of his mother? But it was such a relief that I just kind of sank into it. I've heard people say that they lose themselves in a kiss. But in that moment, it was the opposite for me. I felt like I found myself. Not who I wished I was, or who I was afraid of becoming, but who I really was.

Finally, she managed to escape my grasp. I hadn't realized I'd been holding her so tight. She stepped back and looked at me kind of bewildered.

"Wow," was all she said, then she smiled, turned, and walked to her front door.

I watched her enter and shut the door behind her. Then I turned and walked back to the Boat.

As I pulled away, Mom said, "Well, that was very—"

"If you say sweet," I interrupted, "I'm gonna hurl."

"I was going to say that was very dashing."

"Dashing?" I said. "I kinda like the sound of that."

A quiet smile curled up on her bruised lips. "I thought you might."

That night after dinner, Mom looked at herself in the mirror for the first time. She stared for a while at her half-shaved head, her black eye, and the glittering line of staples.

"Looks like I'm going to have to invest in a lot of hats," she said quietly. Then a strange expression came on her face and she pulled the half-head of hair back. She squinted her one good eye. "Or maybe," she said, "I'll just shave the whole thing and start fresh."

"That would be awesome," I said.

"Yeah." She smiled. "I think so too."

She had bruises all over her body as well, so she had a hard time moving around. I helped her into bed and brought her a glass of water.

"You know, Mom, if you think you need help tomorrow, I could stay home from school."

"Nice try, Sammy. No, I'll be just fine. And anyway, you know the rules. No extracurriculars that day if you aren't in class. And you have that Battle of the Bands thing tomorrow night."

"Oh, I don't think I'll be doing that," I said.

"Samuel," she said, using that rarely invoked Mom Authority voice for the second time. "You are going to compete in that contest. End of story."

16

I could tell nobody knew how to talk

about what had happened. I couldn't blame them. I didn't really know how to talk about it either. There was still this weird sort of distance, like at the hospital. I think everyone was being careful with me or something. Like I was suddenly this feeble person. Like I was helpless.

I could tell it threw them even more when I asked how everyone felt about the contest. We were sitting around a table eating lunch and everybody froze, food halfway to their mouths.

"You mean you still want to do it?" asked Rick.

"Sure," I said.

"What about your mom?" asked TJ.

"She was the one who convinced me, actually." I turned to Joe. "Do you have the lyrics memorized?"

"Of course," he said. "I'm ready if Rick is ready."

We all looked at Rick.

"Let's do it," he said.

The contest was being held at Newport Music Hall, a huge space that usually hosted all the big-name bands on tour. Not the superstar bands, of course. They played at the stadium. But everyone else played at Newport Music Hall. There was a big sunken pit in front, then more dance floor in the back. It also had a whole second mezzanine level with real theater seats. It could seat more than a thousand people. I couldn't even imagine what a thousand people might look like. Actually, I chose not to.

We had to show up right after school to get our names on the list, and we had to bring our gear with us. The nice thing was that we got to park in the reserved parking lot behind the building. KLMN was also providing a lot of other gear, like the amps, speakers, mics, and a simple, bare-bones drum kit so it wouldn't take much time to switch between bands. We even got a sound check to get used to the space. Although the guy who was running it, some gnarly old dude covered in tattoos and sporting a braided goatee that hung halfway down his chest, said it would sound a lot different when the place was filled with people.

Walking out on that stage was amazing. I looked at the seats all the way on the upper level in the back, and they seemed so far away. There was so much space to fill up with music. It almost made me dizzy thinking about it. But a good kind of dizzy, like riding a roller coaster.

"You got three minutes, boys," said the sound-check guy.

We quickly plugged in and ran through our first song. I couldn't believe how great it sounded. We could be as loud as we wanted, and Joe knew the lyrics and Rick played the correct bass line without anyone reminding him. Laurie, Alexander, and Jen5 stood down in the pit cheering and laughing. It was perfect.

We were all grinning like idiots as we walked off the stage.

Rick turned to me and put his hand on my shoulder. "Holy shit, dude," he said. "We might actually do this!"

I just nodded my head. I *knew* we would.

So many bands were playing that they couldn't all fit in the dressing rooms backstage. We ended up getting put in one of the backstage offices. It was dark and kind of cramped with the four of us, plus another band that I didn't recognize. But whatever. We were still backstage at the Newport. Hell, yeah.

"Did you hear the way your bass sounded with that amp?" asked TJ. "Incredible."

"I know, right?" I said. "You could, like, feel it in your stomach it was so intense."

"Yeah," said Rick. "That kit is awesome too."

"That's what happens when you can afford to spend a little money on decent heads," agreed TJ. "Playing it felt great."

"Are you guys glad I thought of this or what?" asked Joe.

The three of us just kind of smiled at him for a moment, because it was a weird thing to say. But he was right. This had been his idea from the start.

"Totally," I said. "You were so right."

There was a stage monitor hooked up in the office so we could hear the other bands play during the competition. At first, all we could hear was the stagehands setting things up. Then the sounds of an audience began to filter through the monitor. At first it was just a low mumble of voices, but it kept growing louder, filling up until it was more like a constant buzzing, as maybe a thousand people talked and laughed at once. We'd already had our sound check, and listening to that audience was our reality check. We were still smiling, but there was a tension to it. And we weren't talking as much.

And then the announcer must have come onstage because the cheers over the monitor rattled the speaker cone.

"Hey, hey, hey!" he yelled into a mic dripping with reverb. "Are you people ready to pick Columbus's best band?"

SCREAM!

"Well, KLMN 103.1 wants—no, they *need*—their faithful listeners to find them a diamond in the rough! They're begging you! Pleading with you!"

"Could this guy be any more cheesy?" Joe groaned.

"Find the next big thing!" continued the announcer.

SCREAM!

"Ten bands, all born and bred right here in this town."

"Sammy, weren't you born in Cleveland?" Rick asked with a nervous grin. "Uh-oh, I hope that doesn't disqualify us."

The announcer continued: "They're young, they're hopeful, and one of them is going to get serious radio play!"

SCREAM!

"Here's what happens. There's going to be three rounds. In the first, they'll each play one song, and you'll pick the top three by cheering as loud as you can for the one you like. And I mean loud and long and out of control. Let us hear it!"

SCREAM!

"Then, the next two rounds will eliminate one band each round until we have our new big thing!"

SCREAM!

"Are you ready?"

I Hate Rock 'n' Roll

SCREAM!

"Then let's hear it for our first band, Cog!"

There was a lot of feedback and general noise at first, but then a pounding, grindcore sound emerged and the band kicked in. It was total speed metal. Not my thing at all, but I had to admit that they were really tight. And like all thrash songs, it was short. It ended crisp and clean like an Olympic diver entering the water.

"Yikes," muttered Rick.

The announcer said, "Let's hear it for Cog!"

SCREAM!

"And now our next band, Casanova Trio!"

SCREAM!

"Oh, God," said Joe. "Poser emo crap."

But it was worse than that. It was cheesy Britpop. It was Wallflowers meets Morrissey.

There was a knock on the door.

"You're next," said a gruff voice.

"We'll sound amazing compared to these pussies," said Joe.

We opened the door and trooped up the dark, narrow stairwell. At the top we entered into the wings. We could see Casanova Trio out onstage, looking just as sad and lame as we had imagined they would.

We could also see the audience.

It's easy to say "one thousand people." But it's not easy to look at them all at once. I got through an audience of fifty at the open mic, but you didn't have to count to see the difference. It was a wall of eyes, all of them about to turn toward us in a few moments. Sick dread flushed through my stomach and my hands were suddenly shaking.

"I think I'm going to throw up," TJ said.

"Shut up," said Joe.

That didn't help at all and TJ sprinted back down the stairs to the bathroom. He came back up a minute later, a little pale but looking much happier.

"You guys should try that," he said. "Seriously."

But even if any of us wanted to, we couldn't. The song ended and we could hear the announcer say, "Let's hear it for Casanova Trio!"

SCREAM!

"And now, show the love for Tragedy of Wisdom!"

SCREAM!

My first thought was, *God, I still hate that name.* But then it was time to walk onstage and that thought evaporated. In fact, all thought evaporated. My stomach totally bottomed out and it was the same feeling as at the open mic. Walking across that stage to my spot seemed like it took forever. My body was so stiff, I felt like Frankenstein's monster. When I got to the right place, just picking up the cord and plugging in my guitar seemed like a huge undertaking. How the hell was I going to play? Then I looked out at the audience—all those faces, all that noise—and for a split second I froze completely. My eyes couldn't hold what I was looking at. My brain was blowing fuses all over the place. If there had been an EKG monitor hooked up to my heart, all you would have heard was *beeeeeeeeeeeeep!*

But I heard the click of TJ's sticks counting us in and even though my head was still on ice, my body knew exactly what to do and started without the rest of me. We were halfway through the first verse before I even realized we were playing.

And it was going brilliantly. We were on. The music pounded through me and I just let it come, let it blast out into the open air. We filled that vast space. Filled it with the music that we had created. I felt like I was ripping open my chest to the audience, showing them everything I had inside. I felt like they knew me, understood me, each and every one of them, and I had nothing to hide. I felt drunk and amazed. This was why I did it. This was why it was all worth it. This was better than anything.

Then we hit the bridge. That's when Joe forgot his lyrics. He kept singing, but he was saying nonsense words. Scatting like some sort of punk rock Ella Fitzgerald, except badly. I looked over at him and I could tell he was getting upset. But maybe we could make it through, get back to a chorus, something he knew, and maybe no one would notice. I glanced over at TJ and Rick, though, and the looks they were giving Joe would have definitely alerted anyone paying attention that things were not going as planned.

And that was when the bass line went somewhere else. Rick seemed so amazed at Joe's scatting routine that he hadn't even realized he'd switched to the wrong song. But Joe noticed. I guess he was glad there was someone else to blame besides himself because he stopped scatting and started talking: "That's our crappy bassist, Rick!" he called to the crowd, mimicking the announcer's cheesy voice. "Never knows what song he's playing! And I always thought fags were supposed to be *good* at music! And while I'm at it, I might as well introduce the rest of the band. TJ, our pussy drummer! He stole my girl with his nice-guy act but was too much of a wimp to tell me! Let's here it for pussy drummers!"

There were a thousand people watching us. Some of them where kind of laughing but a lot of them looked like they didn't know what the hell was going on. All I could think was: Just finish the damn song. Just get to the end and it'll all be over.

"And that, of course, is our guitarist and songwriter, Sammy," said Joe. "And I have to say that this kid has had a rough life. I mean, his mom is so hot that even with twenty staples in her head she gave me a boner. Who knows? Now that I'm single and she's single, hell, maybe I could be Sammy's new daddy!"

That was the moment I stopped playing and threw my guitar at him.

It missed, of course. Guitars aren't very good projectile weapons. It hit the floor and the neck cracked. That sound faded to complete silence. No music, no Joe, no announcer, no audience. My footsteps echoed as I picked up my broken '61 Gibson SG reissue and walked off the stage, through the wings, down the stairwell, out the exit, through the parking lot, and to the Boat.

And I just started driving.

The Moon and Antarctica

17

I never really made the decision. In fact, I don't think I was even paying attention as I drove. But I ended up at Gramps's place. If anyone would understand what I was feeling right then, it was him. But of course he wasn't there. He was in a psych ward, probably never to be released. Because he wasn't going to get better.

Shit.

I sat there in the car and stared at the front lawn of the apartment building. It wasn't very big. Just a little patch of grass spotted with a few dandelions. Less than two weeks ago, Gramps and I sat out there, talking about Chet Baker and the moon. Less than two days ago, he nearly beat my mother to death in probably about the same spot.

I looked down in the passenger seat at the pieces of my

precious '61 Gibson SG reissue. I was mad at Joe for making us all look like complete assholes, but I was just as mad at myself for the way I reacted. It made absolutely no sense to me that my retaliation against him was to break one of the only material objects I cared about. It had just been stupid, meathead rage. Throw whatever was in my hands at the guy. It didn't look fixable, and there was no way I could afford a new one.

Maybe this was a sign. Here I was, no guitar, no band. Maybe I should just forget the whole thing and become a math geek or something. Maybe then I wouldn't be such a angsty little tool. Maybe then I wouldn't go crazy like Gramps. What did he know, anyway? Reach for the moon . . . He was probably already crazy when he said that. Just babbling.

I looked up at the moon. I could see it between the rooftops, big and fat and kind of an orange color. Maybe the craters lined up differently that night, or maybe it was the mood I was in, but I swear I could almost see the man in the moon. But he didn't look like some wise old man, like Gramps said. He didn't look kindly or jolly or any of that. He looked sad and tired, his mouth hanging open like he was a split second away from crying. Maybe he'd looked happier before Neil Armstrong stepped on his face. Or maybe he'd gotten depressed because he had to stare down at us all the time.

Or maybe I was just looking at it wrong. Maybe what

Ms. Jansen had said was right. Things happened that you couldn't control. But you could always choose how you dealt with them.

This was the "shit pile," after all. The stuff that Gramps said was a musician's job to make beautiful. I didn't know if I really touched the moon like Gramps said, but I felt *something* at that open mic. I had taken all my fear and all Jen5's stress, and I had turned it into something that maybe made everybody's night just a little better. And even tonight, when we first started to play, it was something really amazing. Something that was more than just Sammy Bojar.

I couldn't stop playing music. Even if I knew I would never be famous. Even if I had to work at a coffee shop and play a friggin' cigar box strung with wire, I'd still play music. Because I knew I wanted that feeling again. I'd do just about anything to get it.

I was doomed, maybe. But by choice.

I wasn't ready to tell my mom what had happened yet, so I drove over to Jen5's house. I had been sitting in my car for a while in front of Gramps's, so I hoped she'd aleady be home from the concert. But when I knocked on the door, Mr. Russell answered.

"Sorry it's so late, Mr. Russell," I said. "Is Jennifer around?"

One of his bushy white eyebrows slowly raised.

"No, she isn't here. I thought she was with you."

"Yeah . . . I left early."

"Would you like to come in?" he asked suddenly.

"Oh, uh . . ." I couldn't think of a polite way to say no, so I nodded. "Sure, thanks."

"You had some sort of music contest this evening, didn't you?" he asked as we walked to his study.

"Yeah," I said.

"I take it from your tone it didn't go well."

"It was terrible." I sat down heavily in one of his uncomfortable chairs. "I was such an idiot. I thought for sure this band was going to be brilliant. I thought if I just worked hard enough, I could make it all happen. I could . . . I don't know, force it to be good. It could have been, you know? I had it all in my head. The gigs, the album covers, the band photos, even the stupid T-shirts. I could see it like it already existed. But we couldn't even get through a single gig without a major disaster. I see it now, though. Of course, like always, I see it clearly after it's too late. Now it's so obvious that nobody else saw what I saw in the band. No one else believed in it. And no matter how much I believed, everybody in a band has to be playing the same song. You know what I mean?"

I sat and picked at the leather armrest, thinking about how stupid I'd been. How everyone had been telling me, but I just hadn't listened.

"So the band has broken up?" asked Mr. Russell.

"Yeah," I said. "And so has my guitar."

"What?"

"Another idiot thing I did. I just got so angry. At Joe for being such a dick. At Rick for being such a slacker. I don't know, it was like I couldn't think right and I just . . . threw my guitar at Joe. Broke the neck in half."

"What kind of guitar?" asked Mr. Russell.

"Gibson SG," I said. "Sixty-one reissue."

"A shame," he said. "That's a nice guitar."

"I know," I said.

We sat there for a while, totally quiet. It slowly dawned on me that I had just unloaded on Jen5's dad, of all people. I looked at him now, and I couldn't tell if he was fine with it or not. He just sat there, staring off into space, maybe lost in some deep, poetic thought or something. Maybe he hadn't even been paying attention. Just as well.

Then suddenly he stood up with a sharp intake of breath. He nodded stiffly and said, "Please excuse me for a moment." He walked out of the room so quickly, I wondered if he was going to be sick or something.

I knew I should go home. By now, someone had probably told Mom what had happened anyway, so she'd be up worrying about me. And she could barely get around. If I was any kind of good son, I'd be taking care of her right now. As soon as Mr. Russell got back, I'd say good night and head home.

Except when Mr. Russell came back, he was carrying a guitar case. It was a big, black, old hard-shell case.

"Here," said Mr. Russell, holding it out to me. "I'd like you to have this."

"Mr. Russell . . . I can't—"

"Please." He held up a hand like a traffic cop. Then he held the case out to me again. "Open it."

I took the case and placed it on my lap. I popped the tarnished brass latches and opened the lid. Inside was a big, wooden, hollow-bodied electric.

"Is this? . . . ," I said.

"A Gibson ES-175," said Mr. Russell. "It was actually a custom for a jazz guitarist named Joe Pass."

"Joe Pass? He played with Oscar Peterson a lot, right?" I asked. "And I think Ella Fitzgerald?"

Mr. Russell broke out into a huge smile. "Yes, that's absolutely correct, Samuel."

"And this was his actual guitar?" I asked.

"Yes," he said.

I held it out to him. "Mr. Russell. This is way too nice for me. I don't—"

"Guitars are meant to be played, not collected. It's yours now."

I carefully picked it up and put the case to the side. The guitar had real weight to it. It felt like a presence. Like a person, really. I know that if you don't love guitars, that makes no sense, but trust me. There are some things that just feel different.

I propped it up on my lap and lightly ran my fingers across the strings. Even without being plugged in, you could tell this was the real deal. The sound vibrated through the wood with a thick, earthy hum. I felt like I really shouldn't accept the gift. But I couldn't help myself. Once I heard that sound, I couldn't put it down. I had to hear more. So I just started playing, light and quiet, no distortion, no amp, no nothing. Just me, some strings, and some wood. The body of the guitar was so big, I felt like I was hugging it. And when I pressed it close, the sound passed from the back of the guitar into my chest. This was different from just emptying out the angst. I was letting something back in at the same time. I wasn't just playing the guitar, I was having a conversation with it. It was wise. And kind. Like someone's grandfather.

I don't know how long I played, but it must have been a while. At some point, Mr. Russell slipped out of the room. Then Jen5 came home.

"Hey," I said, and started to smile. But I stopped when I saw her tense expression.

"This is where you've been?" she demanded, her voice higher pitched that usual. "Hanging out with my dad?"

"I was looking for you. . . . And then—"

"Okay, you have to call your mother. She's totally freaking out!"

"What? Why?"

"Um, maybe because it's midnight and you've been missing for *hours*?"

"You thought I was missing?" I asked as I carefully put the guitar back in its case.

"Me, Rick, TJ, Alex, Laurie—we've been looking everywhere for you. It was like a freaking dragnet, with Rick and my friend Zeke in your mom's car, TJ and Laurie in his little Fiesta, and me and Alex in his Jeep. I just stopped at home to tell my dad we were scouring the entire city looking for you so he wouldn't worry about me."

"Pause for a second," I said. "Rick and Zeke?"

She flashed a wicked grin. "Totally my doing. Rick will probably hate me for it, but whatever. The point is, we were all totally flipping out."

"Why?"

"Well," she said, suddenly looking a little unsure of herself.

"What with everything that's happened the past few days, we were worried you'd do something stupid . . ."

"What, like kill myself or something?"

"No!" she said. "Well, okay, the thought did cross my mind. But that's not . . . I was just . . ." Then she shook her head and frowned. "I am allowed to be worried about you whenever I want. I don't need excuses." Then she crossed her arms like a little kid.

I couldn't help myself. I walked over and grabbed her face in my hands and kissed her.

"Sorry," I said quietly, still holding her chin in my hand. "I didn't realize . . ."

"Yeah, well, just call your mom," she said, jamming a pink cell phone in my face, "before she has to go *back* to the hospital."

It took me a while to calm my mom down and to assure her that I was just at Jen5's house and I would be home in only a few minutes. In fact, I could have driven back and forth between our houses three times before I was finally able to get off the phone.

"I guess I better get home," I said to Jen5 as I picked up the guitar.

"Wait," said Jen5, her voice getting quiet, like she didn't want anyone else to hear. "He gave you that?"

"Uh, yeah," I said. "I told him no, but he wouldn't listen."

"Wow, that's like his favorite collector's piece ever." She stared at it, then at me, then back at the guitar. A slight smile started to sneak in, but she shook her head. "He really gave you that, huh?"

"Is . . . that cool?" I asked.

"Yeah, please." She waved her hand. "To me, it's one less thing cluttering up this house." Then that smile came back. "It's just nice that my boyfriend and my dad actually get along. I don't know why. It just is."

I gave her another quick kiss and tried to leave, but she pulled me back.

"Hey," she said. "You okay?"

"Yeah," I said. "I think I am, actually."

"Jeez, if I'd known all it would take to make you happy was a fancy guitar, I would have taken up a collection years ago."

"Ha," I said, then kissed her again. Just because.

Mr. Russell was in the kitchen, making tea.

"Hey, uh, thanks again, Mr. Russell. For the guitar. I don't know how I can ever make this up to you."

He smiled slightly and said, "Just don't hurl it at any tyrants. Yes?"

"Sure thing, Mr. Russell. Sure thing."

As I was leaving Jen5's house, I noticed a Jeep parked in front that looked a lot like Alexander's. I walked over to it, and sure enough, there he was, sitting at the wheel, playing "Ode to Joy" in hand farts.

"Hey, I'm found," I said.

"Oh, hey, Sammy. Great. I guess I should go home now or something."

"It's pretty late," I agreed.

"Sorry about tonight," he said. "That sucked."

"You know what?" I said. "Forget about it." Then I leaned into the window a little. "Hey, you know, I have this crazy idea. You want to start a band with me and TJ?"

"Me? In a band?" He seemed genuinely amazed by the idea. Like he had never thought of it before. "Sure!" Then he thought about it. "Uh, playing bass, right?"

"Yeah, Alex. Bass."

"Oh, good," he said. "I've still got some work before I'm ready to perform my hand farts for the general public."

"Maybe you could just have like one little solo or something," I said.

"You think so?"

"Totally."

So Far I Have Not Found a Science

18

We decided to call our band Fidgeting.

Alexander, TJ, and I talked about it for hours. And I mean *talked*. There was no yelling, no threats, no kicking over trash cans. We talked all night long, wrote up lists, laughed, and drank way too much coffee. All three of us had statements we wanted to make, but we quickly realized that the statements were limiting and didn't really give the listener an impression of our sound. So we decided that a descriptive word would be best.

"But an active word too," said TJ. "Something that does something to the listener."

"Alex! Quick!" I said. "How do you feel right now?"

"Uh . . . fidgety?" said Alexander, most likely because he'd had about ten cups of coffee.

"Yeah," said TJ. "Fidgeting . . ."

And it just felt right.

In fact, everything about the band just felt right. I never realized how hard things had been with Tragedy of Wisdom until I found out how easy it could be. Writing songs was completely different. I would just write the lyrics and guitar part, bring those in, and Alexander and TJ would figure out what went with it way better than I ever could have. And since I was doing most of the singing, I didn't have to worry about whether it fit in with someone else's voice. It was my own voice now.

I'd like to say that Joe and I had a big confrontation or fight or something. After all, he did say that stuff about my mom. But we didn't. In fact, we didn't even really talk after that. I saw him sitting by himself at lunch and he still looked tough and scary and mean. But no matter what, now I always saw that sad, slumped guy who knew what the inside of the ER looked like way too well. Everyone who'd ever tried to be his friend, he just pushed away. Pissed them off or beat them up or whatever. I mean, nobody had been as nice to him as I had. Nobody had given him as many chances. And he was still a total asshole to me. I wondered what it took to make a guy like that. Maybe he was just born a jerk. But I don't think so. I think life pulled some serious shit on him. Way worse than anything I'd ever experienced. And knowing that, I guess all I could feel for him was pity. So I just left him alone.

I think that was probably the meanest thing I could have done anyway.

The part that I thought would be the hardest was telling Rick he wasn't invited to come along to the new band. But as it turned out, he was relieved.

"I think we both know I suck at playing bass," he said.

We were at Idiot Child on a Saturday afternoon. Rain was pouring down the front bay windows like a waterfall as we nestled into old easy chairs. The place felt warm and cozy, with a mellow folk song by Iron and Wine whispering over the speakers.

"But you could be a good bassist," I said. "If you wanted to be. If you tried harder."

"Maybe," he said. "But I don't want to. I don't enjoy it. Not like you do. In fact, I was already thinking of quitting before the contest. I could tell I was letting you down."

"You weren't—"

"Sammy," he said. "You suck at lying. I was letting you

down and I guess I was . . . I don't know, starting to worry that it was messing up our friendship."

"So you were going to quit the band to save our friendship?"

"Seemed like a good reason at the time. So this all works out for the best. I'll just be a groupie like Fiver and Laurie." Then he pulled a cigarette out of his pocket and lit it.

"When did you start buying your own smokes?" I asked.

"I quit the bass. Had to take up something, right? And I was at this club last night and smoking gave me something to do."

"You?" I said, unable to keep the shock out of my voice. "*You* were at a club?"

"Yeah," Rick said, and blew a puff of smoke.

"A *gay* club?"

"Yes!" he snapped. "But I didn't dance or anything."

"Did you go alone?"

He scratched the back of his head uncomfortably. "Asshole, I knew you were going to ask me that . . ."

"Well?"

"No, of course not. Zeke dragged me there. Do you really think I would choose to go to a club?"

"Zeke, huh?" I asked.

"Okay, okay, don't rub it in," he said. "It was just . . . I mean, Joe basically outed me in front of the entire Columbus music scene. And I mean, you guys are great and all, but it was nice to have someone there that night who understood what that might feel like."

"And?" I said.

"And, yeah, once I gave him a chance, he was a really cool guy."

"And?"

"Shit, dude. Do you want me to tell you we made out or something?"

"Actually," I said, "yeah. Because friends should be able to tell each other stuff like that and it isn't weird."

"Fine! You win! I'm totally in love with him and I want us to go on double dates with you and Fiver! Happy now?"

"Yes," I said.

A couple of weeks later, Mom, Jen5, and I went to visit Gramps at the nursing home.

"Assisted living," Mom corrected me during the drive there.

She had gone for the shaved look, and it really did look awesome. It seemed to give her a sharpness and energy I hadn't seen in her before. For some reason, Rick, Alexander, and TJ all felt the need to inform me that she still looked hot, even bald.

"What's the difference between a nursing home and assisted living?" asked Jen5 from the front passenger seat.

"A nursing home is more like a hospital," said Mom. "Assisted living tries to be a little more like a real life. Gramps has a roommate, but they actually have real beds and a common living room and dinning room. And I found one that has a piano."

We sat in silence for a minute. Then Jen5 said, "Ms. B, are you mad at your father?"

Mom was quiet for a moment, then she said, "Yes, I am. But not because he beat me over the head with a wrench." Then she laughed loudly.

Jen5 looked at me. "I don't get it."

"Welcome to my world," I said. "Therapist humor."

The place felt like the community center where Tragedy of Wisdom used to rehearse. Flat brown carpet, beige walls, lots of little rooms. I had a feeling there wasn't a dance studio, though.

At the front desk, we had to get checked off a list and then buzzed through a security door.

"The entire building is locked down," Mom explained as we walked down a brightly lit hallway. "Otherwise, some of them would wander off."

So Far I Have Not Found a Science

Then we walked into a huge room. At the far end were a bunch of cafeteria tables just like at school. Some of the old people were sitting there drinking coffee, talking to one another or to themselves. They all seemed very mellow. Or drugged. I don't know what I'd been expecting. I guess strait-jackets and creepy orderlies all in white. But except for the fact that the doors were electronically sealed and no one was smoking, it was more like a bingo hall.

To the left of the cafeteria was a big TV. A lot of other old people where lounging in chairs around it, watching Animal Planet. To the right was a nice little Spinnaker piano. And playing the piano was Gramps.

He seemed peaceful and content as he played his old favorite, "I'm Beginning to See the Light," but his playing was different somehow. None of his normal trills or embellishments or crazy runs that he used to do. It was just the song itself, simple and even a little stiff, like he was playing from sheet music, although there wasn't anything in front of him and if there was one song he knew by heart, it was that one. I could see his lips moving. At first I thought he was singing along to the song, but as we got closer, I realized he was actually reciting random lines from a bedtime story he used to read to me when I was little called *Goodnight Moon*.

"*Goodnight noises everywhere*," I could hear him sing to himself as we got close.

Mom cleared her throat. "Dad?" she said. "How are you?"

Gramps continued to play as he looked at us. His voice was very soft and mild as he said, "Good God, girl, what happened to your head?"

"Latest fashion, Dad," said Mom drily. "Gotta keep up with the times."

He laughed and kept playing. After a moment, he said, "You're a pretty girl. My daughter Sarah. She's a pretty girl too. Do you know her?"

"Yeah," she said, and I could see her struggling not to show the hurt. "I know her."

"Like this one," said Gramps. He nodded his head toward Jen5 while still playing. "I can tell just by looking at her. Spitfire!" He chuckled. Then his face suddenly got a little pouty, like a cranky toddler.

"Where the hell is Sammy?" he said.

"Right here, Gramps," I said.

"Damn, boy, can't you see I need some help here? I'm old and crazy and can't remember the words to this song! How's it start?"

I looked around the room sheepishly. It felt a little

weird. Although no one seemed to even notice that we were there.

"Well?" he said. "I can't vamp forever!"

So what else could I do? I started singing:

"I never cared much for moonlit skies. I never wink back at fireflies."

Gramps cackled gleefully and started pounding the keys and added his own quavering voice to mine.

"But now that the stars are in your eyes, I'm beginning to see the light!"

He insisted we sing through the entire song. When it was finished, he was all smiles and nods. "Thank you," he said. Then his face began to glaze over and he mumbled, "I think I'd like to rest now."

He got unsteadily to his feet and, without saying good-bye, lurched off to his room.

We looked at each other awkwardly.

"Come on, kids," Mom said. "Let's go."

After we'd dropped Jen5 off, we drove home in silence. When we got to the house, Mom parked the car, but she didn't get out. Instead she just sat there and stared out the window.

"You and Gramps . . . have something . . . that I

never did," she said. "You share something. I don't really understand it, but I know it can lead people to dangerous places. It's that thing that took my mother away. It's the thing that can ruin not only your own life, but the lives of those you love."

She sat there for a moment still staring straight ahead, and I was sure that some really bad news was about to hit me. I could practically taste it in the air.

"But," she said, "that thing, whatever it is, also makes life so much better. What just happened with you and Gramps . . . to me, that was beautiful. And I think that sometimes I try to put my own fears and distrust of this thing on you . . ." She just kind of trailed off, still staring out the window. "And that isn't right. So, I'm sorry."

I realized that I'd been holding my breath.

"So . . . ," I said after a while. "Does this mean I can be a professional musician?"

She smiled. Then she chuckled. Then she full on laughed out loud. "Sure, Sam. Sure. But you still have to go to college."

So, tonight Fidgeting had our first real gig. We even got paid for it. Okay, it was at a pizza shop down by the college campus. And we got paid in pizza. But whatever. Because the thing is, we opened for Monster Zero.

So Far I Have Not Found a Science

Eric Strom had some friend in the Battle of the Bands contest, so he saw the Tragedy of Wisdom train wreck and remembered me from the coffee shop. Then, through some chain of people I never fully understood, he ended up at some party that Fidgeting was playing. He recognized me again and came over. He gave me some shit about breaking my ax at the Battle of the Bands, and then we started talking music and how he wanted to start building the local scene now that they actually had a little bit of clout around town. They wanted to start having new bands open for them, just a couple of songs to warm up the crowd, and he liked our sound, so were we interested? Well, after Jen5 picked me up off the floor, I said yes, of course.

I'm not going to lie. When the day of the gig finally arrived, I was terrified. This wasn't just my friends from school. This was college students and adults, and somehow that seemed official. More real. I wasn't totally over my fear of singing in front of people. It was always just on the edge of becoming a problem every time we played in front of people.

We started with a song that Alexander and I cowrote called "Theodore the Vampire." It's a perky, upbeat song (Alex's influence) about a vampire who is lonely because he keeps killing all his friends (my influence). It has a weird dark/light sound that people seem to really connect to. Plus it has this peppy chorus that goes:

> *But he never has 'em for too long*
> *Things always seem to turn out wrong*
> *His tummy starts to get hungry*
> *And he can't help but kill them all!*

It loses something on paper. But trust me, it's hilarious when Alexander and I sing it into a single mic like doo-wop girls or something. And it features a hand-fart solo. Seriously. It's just for eight bars of music, but we cut everything else, so it's just Alex, *phfip-phopping* into the mic in dead silence, then we go crashing back into the chorus.

Anyway, I was wound pretty tight with that campus crowd watching, and about halfway through the song, my voice started going out on me. My throat was just so dry from nerves that it came out squeakier and squeakier until by the time the song was over, I was barely making a sound. But then, some random dude that I had never met before just walked up to the stage and handed me his soda. Thinking about it now, it was like in some cheesy TV commercial, but at the time, I was just so grateful. And kind of surprised.

Right up until that moment, I guess I always thought of

a performer's relationship to an audience almost like it was a conflict, like they were just waiting to expose me for the wannabe poser that I was. Maybe that was why I always got so nervous. But in that moment, I realized that a lot of people didn't actually think of me as a wannabe. They weren't really judging me at all. They just wanted to hear some good music, and hoped I could provide it. They were just looking for a little of that reach-for-the-moon magic. It was that simple.

Whether it was the soda or that realization, my voice was fine for the rest of the set. In fact, Eric asked if we were interested in opening for them again, and maybe even doing a mini tour with them during the summer.

I don't know if this is the start of something big or not. And honestly, I don't really care. Well, okay. I care a little. It would be nice to make some real money playing music. And every once in a while, I give in to the stupid little fantasies about album covers and T-shirts. But that's not the main thing. Most of the time, instead of thinking about being a musician, I just play music now.

Sammy's Rock and Jazz Mashup Playlist

(a.k.a. The Soundtrack for This Book)

"Idiots Rule," by Jane's Addiction

"Communist Daughter," by Neutral Milk Hotel

"I'm Beginning to See the Light," by Edward Kennedy "Duke"
Ellington, Don George, and Johnny Hodges

"Someday You Will Be Loved," by Death Cab for Cutie

"Take the Skinheads Bowling," by Camper Van Beethoven

"Wake Up," by Rage Against the Machine

"Only Shallow," by My Bloody Valentine

"Breathe," by Pink Floyd

"How High the Moon," by Nancy Hamilton and Morgan Lewis

"I Just Wanna Get Along," by the Breeders

"Monkey Gone to Heaven," by the Pixies

"Caring Is Creepy," by the Shins

"Wave of Mutilation," by the Pixies

"Haven't Got a Clue," by the Flaming Lips

"Interstellar Space," by John Coltrane

"Yerself Is Steam," by Mercury Rev

"Car Wash Hair," by Mercury Rev

"Just Like Heaven," by the Cure

"La La Love You," by the Pixies

"Taste the Pain," by the Red Hot Chili Peppers

"Summer Sketch," by Russ Freeman

"Overpowered by Funk," by the Clash

"Addicted to Fame," by Subset

"Just Like Honey," by the Jesus and Mary Chain

"Everything in Its Right Place," by Radiohead

"Sins of the Father," by Tom Waits

"Burning Inside," by Ministry

"I Hate Rock 'n' Roll," by the Jesus and Mary Chain

"The Moon and Antarctica," by Modest Mouse

"So Far I Have Not Found a Science," by Soul Coughing

For more music suggestions, go to

strutsandfretsbook.com.

Acknowledgments

There are so many people who were directly or indirectly responsible for the creation of this book. Thank you of course to my agent, Emily Sylvan Kim, who suggested I try my hand at young adult fiction and without whom this story would have remained only a text file on my computer. To my editor, Maggie Lehrman, who pushed this story to a richness I hadn't realized was possible until she pointed it out to me. To Chad W. Beckerman and Melissa Arnst, who somehow conjured up the perfect book design. To Zach Morris, Mark Levine, and Scott Pinzon for their thoughtful criticism and enthusiasm in early drafts. To my mother, Gini, for giving me my first guitar, and my stepfather, Tom, for giving me my first album. To my wife, Gretchen, for her endless support, encouragement, and patience throughout the writing process. And to my sons, Logan and Zane, for being a constant reminder of why I must write.

Lastly, I want to thank the real Tragedy of Wisdom, Fidgeting, Monster Zero, and all the other bands who inspired me back in the day when I made music, as well as all the amazing artists coming out of unexpected places today.

JON SKOVRON

is a music geek who can play nine instruments, but none of them well. This is his first novel. In his spare time, he writes technical manuals and tries to forget about his sordid past as an actor. He lives with his wife and two kids outside Washington, D.C. To learn more about him, the book, or the music, visit him at strutsandfretsbook.com.

This book was art directed

and designed by Chad W. Beckerman. The display type was hand drawn by Melissa Arnst. The text is set in 12-point Adobe Garamond, a typeface based on those created in the sixteenth century by Claude Garamond. Garamond modeled his typefaces on ones created by Venetian printers at the end of the fifteenth century. The modern version used in this book was designed by Robert Slimbach, who studied Garamond's historic typefaces at the Plantin-Moretus Museum in Antwerp, Belgium. The jacket and interior photographs were taken by Jonathan Beckerman.

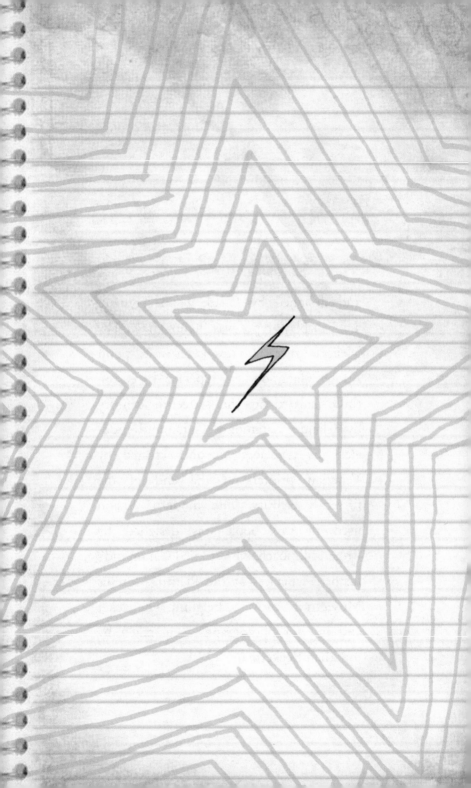